Come Not To Us

D1522132

Come Not To Us

by *Brett Ramseyer*

To Mom for literature and Dad for history

1

"Poot ze gun in your maul!" called a voice.

Peter Sonderling, an accountant, a cuckold, a grieving son, stood in the darkness of the country road, ready to blow himself to hell.

But sometimes when the path burns, a demon can turn animus outward, aversion a virtue, cause him to point the pistol away from his own temple. Only then might he go straight to hell -- *and back* -- sift the ashes to know his past, reclaim his present, find a future direction so as not wander, a lost soul.

***

It is a wonder that anyone can find anything in the Michigan backwoods. It is a place for losing things. Roads meet each other at acute angles then amble languidly like retired farmers walking their wives on silent dawns. They traipse around green covered ponds encircled in reeds, past overgrown fields thick with thistle and over sandy ridges littered with specks of quartz shattered by an ancient glacier. Entire homes and sometimes even roads disappear. This oblivion takes only time.

It is often difficult to pinpoint when the first saplings start to encroach on a byway to make it a track. One from outside can never see definitively if inhabitants of a forest cabin allowed the road to disappear because they never returned home or because they never left. Either way, the structure rots to dust and the foundation crumbles in decades of heavy winters. Myrtle that a couple lovingly planted along the brook now creeps through the living room. A maze of thin stemmed maples searching skyward for light now obscure any hint of a lane where children learned to walk. The only tangible evidence of humanity is the rusted cast iron door of a stove that felt no fire in a half century. Abode and road are quietly divorced forever.

Still, rednecks print off maps at the county courthouse that award them unmerited license to trespass their trucks in search of hunting blinds. It serves a current property owner little to explain that an avenue no longer exists because the average self-assured hunter will wave the map and rave about his American freedom. A curious confidence convinces a man that a few square inches of pulp and ink represent more reality than a forest of lumber that grows in front of him.

Peter needed to muster this kind of confidence to find his way. He had tangled himself into a labyrinth of countryside roads he felt he could not retrace to his life. At every intersection he stomped the accelerator anew in hopes his tires would wrinkle every map in existence. He remembered the night in bitter snapshots that lay scattered over the crimson carpet of his retina. Creating order from face down photos would work if only Peter could turn them over. No one needs remember his last night on earth, unless he wakes up from the nightmare.

***

He pressed the black barrel to his temple and his finger began to pull back the dark crescent of a trigger. The Mercedes headlights projected his vision of tragedy.

My front page story. She'll finally be forced to see what she caused staring back at her in print or on the late news, a long shot with the car and a thick slick of blood mixing with the dust in the road. She'll identify what's left with guilt and explain to the neighbors why and where and how and most importantly the who - who it was - who it should have been.

One lead slug stood in inert anxiety waiting to explode through his troubles like an exclamation point when a call slipped out of the underworld.

"Poot ze gun in your maul!" Peter's front page fluttered to the floor, an unread obituary.

Peter whirled around with rage and staggered into blackness. He waved the gun in front of him threatening like the newly blind. "Who wants to die with me!" he screamed.

"Who vants to die? Not you. A man mit a gun in his maul vants to die," shot back in an even tone from beyond the penumbra of the lights.

Peter pounded his eyes shut to blink away the light. He stepped from the blinding beam and bumped into the ghost who stole the final scripted page of his life. With vision slowly returning, Peter could barely make out an old man leaning precariously on a stick. He raised the gun to the stranger's chest. The ancient figure deliberately turned away from him and began to hobble up the road. "Turn and face your maker!" Peter boiled, but the man did not stop walking.

"No vun vill die tonight. Get ze hell out of here before I call ze police," floated back over his shoulder. Peter brought his hands together and squeezed, looked down, and squeezed again. Nothing. He no longer aimed, but pulled the trigger in staccato succession. The man disappeared into the darkness and Peter hurled the pistol into the night. Chasing quickly behind Peter loosed a primal growl thought lost to humanity after millions of years of evolution, but now it rumbled from his chest.

Peter sprang back to the car with the full intent of running the man down. Still reeling he slammed himself down into the seat and caught his temple on the roof of the car. The sudden pang made him reach for a splitting skull and left him holding his exhausted head in his hands. With this new failure oozing out the side of his head he turned the car and left

Come Not To Us

with his taillights glowing red behind him. He definitely did not make headlines.

***

He never had, not in high school on the sports page or in college when everyone else protested the next great evil sweeping over the nation. The Montgomery Bus Boycott happened in the midst of his oblivious boyhood and Freedom Summer in '64 scared the hell out of him in his dorm lounge at the University of Chicago. He saw all the newscasts when the civil rights workers disappeared in vivid black and white. Peter preferred his easy summer job of working on the donor lists for the new humanities and social science library in his makeshift office. A couple of card tables in a drafty back hallway of Culver Hall did not make for an exciting summer, but the occasional passerby could speed up the clock.

"Hey Pete!" Tony Sciori interrupted on his midmorning twenty-minute stroll to the drinking fountain. Tony, pre-law at U of C, made his summer wage by practicing "The janitorial arts." He deliberately dallied through all breaks garnering skill at stretching his billing hours for when he made his fat law practice in the suburbs. He saved his energy for the Neanderthal pursuits of lifting heavy things to harden his athletic body for the ladies. "D'you see the latest on Mississippi last night?"

Peter looked up from his latest fund raising figures, "Yeah, racism is rearing its ugly head once again."

"How do you know that? Three guys are missing. There still isn't word what happened to them yet. They were just Negroes anyway. In my math the world minus three Negroes equals a plus three for society."

I knew it was an ugly head, but I didn't know it was your head. "They weren't all black. Two of them were white, how do you think it made national news?"

"Oh yeah, I saw that - but those guys were Jewish." Tony spit into the fountain and bent down to wet his lips. On his way back a sparkle of merriment lit up his eye. "Well then I guess my math was wrong. In that case the world minus a Negro and two kikes equals plus five." His laugh echoed through the hard empty hall and hit Peter soundly on the jaw.

Peter sat motionless atop volcanic pressures. Obsidian hate blinded his pupils to the day. He could only envision Goodman, Chaney, and Schwerner's blank stares on the FBI poster, three college kids risking their lives for voting rights, but they looked like men to Peter. His mind recalled the three faces and settled on Andrew Goodman, twenty, because it bore such a strong resemblance to what Peter saw in his mirror. Goodman's thick, dark eyebrows almost cast shadows on this face and his wave of black hair curled back and made Peter wish for a haircut. The similar face of a man felt too different from the boy who sat alone with his papers in the cool concrete hall.

3

Brett Ramseyer

Peter gathered his things and began to rationalize his summer stay at the University. With his hands full of cardboard boxes, receipts and plans he backed his way out of the heavy wooden double doors only to squint in the mid-day burn of early July. The cool grass covered quadrangle lay quiet and desolate except for two pretty coeds sunning their arms and ankles in front of the Biology Center. Peter lowered his paraphernalia to the steps and nonchalantly lit a cigarette trying to gain the girls' attention. Smoking arose as his latest attempt to look older. His eighteenth birthday arrived in two weeks, but Tony stepped out from the shadows of a tree to talk to the two girls. They squinted in the rays of the sun that still slipped around his thick neck. As he sat beside the blonde girl they both turned away from Peter and his mind slipped quickly back to the image of Andrew Goodman as he scanned up the stories to the sharp gables overhead. He snuck a glance across the lawn and resigned himself to the fact that he waited futilely for notice from the girls.

As he pulled deep at the smoke, the Kent Chemical Laboratory under gray shade caught his attention. *What wonderfully disastrous concoctions might lie beyond those stone walls? If I only had a key I could search the labs for the perfect beaker to drop my cigarette into and start the chain reaction that would level the building. I surely would draw some headlines then, like Goodman.* Even the name made Peter jealous. *Who walks around introducing themselves as, A. Good - man.* "Hello. I'm Andrew Goodman." The name commanded etching on the edifice of a bank or even across the quadrangle peeking out from behind the old growth ivy.

Instead, Sonderling.

Peter Sonderling could think of nothing powerful, successful or revered that sounded remotely like Sonderling. *Changeling, foundling, cradling. All about children.... What is something strong? Masculine? Calling, falling, bawling. No, still kids – kids. Heckling – tackling, yes tackling! It's football, athletic and tough.* And then Peter remembered his last football game, fifth grade recess after lunch. He remembered tackling and the hot garlic puffs of breath from Max Smolenski in his eye. Peter stopped looking for power in his name. He bent down for his things and walked away from it all.

2

Cold wet smoke rose off the water, divided and raced like spirits toward him. Its morning chill blew through him and he clenched his jaw for warmth. The ducks and swallows played across the pink dawn that changed its shape and color with every passing bird. The early gray clouds shifted orange, pink, gold back down again to a purple mass in a brightening sky. Water's quiet lap intermixed with the lonely haunts of birds that sounded of far off wooden flutes, hollow and shrill. Even frogs awakened from the depths of ooze to sound bi-plane climbing yawns.

Last night's rain brought a freshness to the air that Peter grudgingly pulled in. He stood up from his padded lawn chair to stretch away the soreness of the cottages sagging mattress and felt his dew heavy trunks clinging to him. He tenderly traced out his jutting temple and shook his head. He was not glad to be alive, but he did strain to hear the fisherman mumble that rolled across the water from the middle of the lake. The two coarse voiced men slumped over their reels, but quickened as the orange sun finally crested the shoreline forest.

Peter questioned what could make men rise at five a.m. to troll for cold fish, surely not a food quest. Thick jackets could not hide their ample middles. The sudden sound of excitement escaped from one of the fishermen as he stood in the bow. He arched his back and put a flex on his rod. Peter could feel the hair bristling on his neck as he leaned forward. Short lived anticipation turned mundane as the man missed setting the hook and instead pulled up a tangled salad of sea greens. He cleaned the hook and recast in hopes that the next to surface would die.

Morning murder pulled the poor to the bridges and docksides, the dull middle class to their flat bottom boats, and the rich to their fishing yachts. They could all feel power, mastery, and accomplishment by wrestling the life out of a fish. Disgusted, Peter leered at the spindle-legged heron strutting on the shore. It too brought too much pomp and glory to preying on the unsuspecting and the senseless.

Peter turned and meandered his way back to the cottage. He had no plans for today. Today did not exist for Peter, yet he felt he must do something. Sunday suicide sounded unseemly, but he imagined swimming across the lake to stagger into one of the white-spired churches in town anyhow. He would drip his way to the altar before he would slash his wrists with a paring knife just to see the horror on the washed faces of the congregation. Instead, he only pierced the beautiful shining flesh of an apple. He tried to ignore the mealy texture of the slice of fruit that wintered

Brett Ramseyer

poorly in cold storage and stared blankly at the floor. He tapped the tip of the knife on the countertop in contemplation of action until he heard the cadence he made.

It scared him into alertness, "The Luger!" He could still feel the indentation left by the trigger on his right index finger. *How many times did I pull that trigger?* Its empty thin beat started slowly and quickened to double time before he had hurled it into silence. *Was that old man even there? He couldn't have been. He disappeared so fast and could barely walk. No old man would hobble around in the dark in that wilderness. It must have been a hallucination, but the gun.*

Peter hated to think what could happen. He worried some hiking farm boy traipsing home for lunch could discover it in the weeds only to return some dark night to show off to his girl. *He'll splatter her forehead with his face.* His spiraling mind left two holes dangling below the last button on his light blue oxford. He jumped into his jeans and slid his bare feet into his canvas deck shoes. His keys hid mischievously, so he just bumbled his way through the side door in hopes of finding his spare set in the garage. When he turned around the greater portion of Mrs. Van Duinnen's posterior nearly smacked him in the forehead. With blazing round constancy like the sun she rose every morning to work her terraced strawberry bed. She took the 'straw' in berry seriously and religiously cultivated her stock every spring weaving it in an impenetrable mat of stalks to hold the weeds into submission. The deer quite enjoyed the treat when they would poke their wet noses out of the woods across the road every summer. Peter wondered if she ever tasted a ripe red berry from that garden, but she pressed on relentlessly. She and her husband represented some of the few people who lived on the south side of the lake year round, so she possessed an air of omniscient permanence that lorded over the seasonal occupants of the shore.

She gave a start at the slamming door and stood up as if hinged at the waist. "Well Peter, for pity's sake. You gave me a jolt. I didn't expect to see you up at this time in the morning when you drove home so late last night."

"Oh yeah…" *Hold it together. Slow down.* "With the air so crisp this time of year and no bugs I thought I would head off for a hike in the woods this morning." Peter knew from many side-yard conversations not to directly lie to Mrs. Van Duinnen, partial truths afforded the only chance of escape if he did not want her to know everything about him. It would *be* a walk in the woods after all when he was done with it.

"It *is* a beautiful morning for it. Are you heading across the road?"

"No, I thought I would start with a drive," *I hope I can find my keys or this could be ugly,* "And find someplace new to explore."

6

Come Not To Us

"Oh how nice, you'll be back in time for service somewhere won't you?"

"Last I checked there weren't many synagogues in Oceana County Rita."

"Who needs a synagogue? You're always welcome at the Baptist church in town. Everyone can gain His love. It does a body good to hear the scripture."

"Yes, I'm sure it does, but I have only so much time today before I have to head back to Chicago." With that Peter began to back down the sidewalk toward the garage. "We'll have to talk more next time I come up." He began to turn and make his escape as Mrs. Van Duinnen's salvo of questions continued.

"Where's Doreen and the kids?"

"Back at home. The kids were too busy this weekend to make it. Gotta run. I'll see you on a weekend."

"Remember if you two ever want a night out up here, just ask and I would be happy to..." ricocheted off the corner of the house and missed Peter as he ducked into the garage. *Safe. If only the keys are near.* He ducked his head into the Mercedes and saw them dangling from the ignition. He remembered now stepping into the unlocked loft last night and falling exhausted on one of the kids' beds.

How did that old busybody know when I came in last night I didn't even turn on any lights? He started the car and backed out. *She'll watch the kids, ha. We need the kids to watch us these days. Night out, that's even more funny. Twenty years.*

***

"Hey Sonderling," reverberated through Culver Hall. "It's time for a night out," called Tony.

Peter looked up from his neatly stacked table of figures. "And do what?"

"Shit, I don't know. What do you care? You've been locked in your dorm for two weeks straight. The only time I see you is down here in the dark pushing around that pencil. You need intrigue, excitement. You need double-oh-seven. 'Everything he touches turns to excitement!'"

"Let me guess. You need me along because you can't afford it."

"No, no. You buy the tickets and I'll get the popcorn. That's a fair trade."

"Sure at a nickel a bag, what a deal."

"Aw come on. It's a double feature. *Goldfinger* is sure to be the best picture of 1964 and they're replaying *From Russia With Love*. So really you are getting two movies for the price of one and I will have to supply the popcorn for four hours of heart stopping action and gorgeous women."

"Now some truth. It's ogling women you want."

"Of course! Daniela Bianchi." Tony paused and looked up to conjure her naked image in the back of his tiny reptilian brain. "Would I like to give her the gold finger."

"Sciori you're a sick bastard."

"Well who isn't these days. Whad'ya say?"

"What time?"

At quarter to eight the bus's double doors slid open a block down from a derelict marquee. What bulbs not broken blew their filaments long ago and the owner only found it necessary to replace the flickering fluorescent tubes behind the letter board in this neighborhood. The intentional flicker dimmed attention by shouting, "Already broken," to the street below. Anything that looked too pristine near Packingtown expected to have a beer bottle heaved end-over-end into it. Tonight the sign only read 'BOND'. Tony bounded onto the curb and Peter stepped tentatively down behind him.

"What the hell kind of movie theater is this Tony?"

"It's a scary one. Besides it's cheap."

"Why? Is that guy the ticket-taker?" Peter said as he pointed to a wino who lay passed out in the doorway of a boarded up pub.

"He might be." Tony bent over him to look under the brim of his clay red hat and make eye contact. "Two for the Bond double feature, sir." He gave him two good raps on the shoulder only to knock loose a foul dust into the air.

"Would you leave him alone! He's gonna pull out a knife next," said Peter already halfway to the theater. "And give new meaning to ripping your ticket."

"Pete you are such a pussy. I know the guy. He'll get us in. I just wasn't speaking his language. Bonjour Monsieur! Deux billets s'il vous plaît." A rattling paper bag still clenched to the derelict's chest gave the only answer. "Christ. I think he's dead."

"Com'on. I'm paying for myself and leaving you outside."

"Will you relax? Our dates aren't even here yet."

"What dates?"

"We should wait at the stop to make sure they get off anyway. They'll want to see a familiar face connected to my menacing body to protect them. Otherwise they might just ride through and go home." The bulging veins in Tony's neck still gave evidence of his high school fullback days and he flared them out like a cobra while he talked by squaring his jaw. Peter did not want Tony to know, but he felt safer having him around in this slum.

"What dates?"

Come Not To Us

"Two broads I met after work yesterday. I was giving one of them the full court press in the quad and she said she would only go out with me if I found a date for her friend."

"Is that where I came in?"

"No, I asked Jim and Carl, but they didn't trust me and they didn't like the idea of a blind date. I told them she had a great personality."

"So she's escaped from the pound and your own roommates couldn't trust you. I'm three seconds from a mugging here and I'm paying for four tickets now. Absolutely great!"

"So go home. I can handle two women."

"Even the ugly ones?"

"I never said she was ugly. I can't remember because when I see blonde hair and a tight sweater everything else begins to blur. Let me just say, this goldie is a real broad, broad in all the right places."

Peter shook his head in disbelief of all the leering jokes this fullback cracked. All the while he felt his insides twisting like a wet towel and filling him with a heavy urge that made him sway his weight back and forth between the soles of his feet. He wanted to walk away quickly, but black alleys loomed everywhere and Peter wanted to bury Tony in one of them. He could only think to say, "Do these women have names or am I just supposed to call them blonde broad and brunette broad?"

Down the avenue the next bus rumbled toward them. Peter tried to look preoccupied with his watch when the coach scraped to a stop. Two long haired women stood and stepped through the aisle. "The blonde's name is Ilene, she's mine."

"What about the other?"

"I don't know. I can't remember everything it rhymes with Ilene. Colleen, Darlene, somethin'."

"We should have met them on campus this is ridiculous."

"No way. Did you want to pay their bus fare out here too." Peter finally understood what Tony meant by "scary and cheap." Not only did those adjectives describe Tony and his motives, but unveiled his scurrilous scheme to get laid. Any girl would cling to her date in this whiskey row of saloons, brothels, tenements, and abandoned buildings and surely insist that he escort her home. Peter never gave Tony much credit for intelligence, but his diabolic genius worked with distinct precision.

Ilene sprang off the bus first like a field of wheat that waved in the breeze of her perfume. Peter almost recoiled at the pleasantness of her scent in this land of open stench. She seemed not to notice traveling in an opaque bubble all her own that made her perpetually near-sensed. She gave Tony an overly familiar hug before Peter even focused on the woman behind her and suddenly the world shrank to two hazel spheres.

Ilene caught Peter out of the corner of her eye and perfunctorily put out her hand. Peter took it and she said, "Hello, I'm Ilene Bates and you must be..?"

"Peter," said Tony.

"Peter, let me introduce your date for the evening, Doreen." Ilene handed off Peter to her friend then linked her arm with Tony on her way to the theater. Her head bobbed in front of them with excitement and her laugh rang with dissonance against the rhythmic clank of cars over manhole covers.

"She really knows how to blend in to her surroundings, doesn't she?" said Doreen and Peter chuckled away some of his tension. He glanced back up at those eyes that exuded a new warmth to him, but he fixed his gaze just below hers.

"She's just a tad disproportionate. I think if Ken up there lets go Barbie might tip over. He'll probably be trying that later though." Peter had spoken as a reflex and did not even know he had told a joke until it started in Doreen's midsection and traveled up her spine to shake her shoulders with silent laughter.

Doreen turned with a full smile "She's been tipped by lesser men," and looked directly at Peter. The apples of her cheeks rounded out perfectly and he did not know if it was innocent flirting or a genuine cut at him so he smiled back. She took his arm and began to lead him down the sidewalk. "Just so we're clear," she said authoritatively. "You will be taking me home from this ghetto and there will be no tipping of any kind."

"Yes, General."

"That's General Doreen Feldherr to you soldier."

3

A clear spring day hung over Peter in fawn yellow that he ignored. With each mile he drove in confusion his fists clamped down tighter on the wheel and his teeth began to grind themselves to paste. His stare narrowed and darkened. He focused backward on the only image he could see from last night's failed suicide with any clarity, a golden diamond with seven black letters.

***

Peter called them, "The Seven Black Letters." That title made him feel as morbid as Hawthorne, yet there they hid in the corner of the attic under the wedding album. The letters tied together with a thin piece of black satin ribbon shaped in a bow reminded him how Doreen wrapped the children's Christmas presents. The ribbon drew his attention. His real focus, the leak in the roof slowly worked its way into the ceiling of his bedroom. A rusty circle grew over his head as he slept and he finally found a weekend to climb into the cobwebs to investigate and repair the damage. Only his clumsiness caused the discovery. Searching for the source of the problem he picked up the small bookshelf to move it aside and forgot the pitch of the ceiling as he turned. The top of the shelf caught a slanting stud and spilled the entire contents across the floor.

Peter always admired the look of the gifts under the tree on Christmas morning. Doreen took such care in creating the look of Currier and Ives and Rockwell and he liked that Michael and Claudia never met impediments in the bows as they opened their presents. He delighted in their unbridled avarice. It only took one deft pull of the ribbon and the wrapping paper would fall to the floor like Doreen's black silk bathrobe before she stepped into the shower. Peter pulled the ribbon, read, and suddenly stood naked in "The saddest of all prisons."

***

"Old Man" Martin spent his last days there. He died prostrate on the concrete slab of the drunk-tank in the Oceana County Jail. Such a small number of cells barely constituted a prison, but Martin yelled for his green pick-up as soon as Sheriff Kent Ford checked in on him. He feebly rattled the bars and expectorated an arc between them at his jailor. The oil slick that landed could hardly stain the Sheriff's brown shirt. A plug of tobacco had been rotting in Martin's mouth since midnight when they found him slumped over the wheel of his truck.

"Lemme out of prison, pig!"

Brett Ramseyer

"Teddy. Sit your ass down. You should know where the comfy spots are in that tank." said Ford as he looked sideways over his shoulder.

"It's mornin'. You pulled me in drunk now I'm sober. Rattle that skeleton key over in this here lock."

"Not this time Teddy. You sheared off a fire-hydrant and they had to shut off the water east of State Street. You'll be doing some time now."

Ford wanted to release him. He felt sorry for Teddy and this seemed like the least terrible crime he committed in his life. When the deputy found the body the next day Sheriff drove out to the Martin trailer personally to tell his daughter. He felt like putting on boots to wade through the piles of junk that tried to hide the weeds around the blue and white single-wide. He knocked on the hollow white door that seemed to magically open until he looked down to see Teddy's grand-daughter looking up at him. Her bulging eyes set unevenly in her head. She stood the product of one of Teddy's late night binges. That time he ran over his daughter. In six months little Trina was born, related more closely to her grandpa than any little girl should ever be.

"Is your mommy home?" Only elicited terse vulgarity from the bowels of the trailer hurled at Trina. She only swung open the door and pointed to some curls of smoke rising from the front of a worn out recliner. Dawn Martin rose quickly when she saw the sheriff star shining and pulled her high riding shorts out of her discomfort.

"What you want? I ain't done nothing." The women cuffed Trina on the back of the head. "Git to your room!" The little girl's cleft lip curled into a misshapen 'o' and a noise only to be described as "Ow!" came out, no tears.

"Now Dawn, she didn't do any harm and neither have you. I hate to have to be here like this - I'm here to deliver some sad news. I'm – well I'm sorry, but-"

"He's dead ain't 'e?"

"Your father, yes he died last night in the county jail."

Dawn stuck a trailing cigarette into her face. Ford watched the gray ash grow through her fingers and drop to the floor as she pulled smoke deep into her toes. "Where's his truck?"

"Totaled. He hit a fire-hydrant two nights ago."

"Shit! That old drunk couldn't leave me nothin'." She flicked her butt into a pile of rusted tire rims "Thanks." and she slammed the door.

Kent looked at himself in the rearview mirror of his cruiser. He smoothed his coarse gray hair straight back and set his cap on the passenger seat. "It takes all kinds, Kent. It takes all kinds." He readjusted the mirror in place as a black Mercedes-Benz flashed behind him. He craned back in a double-take and quickly backed out of the dust to follow.

12

Come Not To Us

"Nice, '85 500 SEC. Illinois plate. Probably waxed yesterday." He checked the cars speed and stayed well back. Soon the car turned down a dead end. "Uh-oh, another gawking tourist. He better hope the old German doesn't shoot him.

***

Peter's relief at seeing the bent road sign was not the same as last night's. Then he felt strong with purpose and sure of the outcome. Today the black letters made him flush pink at the failure flooding back to him, but he quickly blanched in the daylight of this place. He no longer knew what lay at the end of this road and the uncertainty landed like loneliness on the back of an ant that followed the familiar scent home to find no hole, no friends, no family.

His car rolled on around the bend and he looked curiously at what he had missed last night. The white farmhouse hidden behind cedars and Norway pine winked out at him. The road that appeared as only a tunnel at midnight opened up into acres of wild grass trimmed in sumac. He drove slowly up the same incline where last night's silver screen suicide showing flew off the reel. This time the only silver flipped and tossed on the undersides of the poplar leaves that hung over the gravel.

Should I get out and look? Peter sat higher in his seat trying to peer ahead to the end of the road. He swayed back and forth squinting into a jungle of new May green. He decided to walk from the car. He remembered hurling the Luger at the man who came from up the road so he picked his way fifty yards ahead and back. His feet pressed prints into the sandy channels where the heavy spring rains raced down the sides of the road before they spilled rocks, twigs and earth into the meadow. He bent low to look under foliage and swung his foot like a scythe over weeds to bend them aside. The high banks around him and creek-bed-road under him showed no signs of disturbance or weapon.

"Damn. How far could I have thrown it?" Never an athlete Peter felt unsure what prowess his adrenaline rage created. At the foot of the hill to his west his eye followed barbed wire rusted black that crested in the trunks of a line of trees and troughed under the earth. Decades of xylem and phloem had pinched their way around an unkempt fence and it reminded him of the wiry arc of a suspension bridge. He wondered if the white pines, walnuts and thorny locusts actually held up this derelict track before it slid off the hill into the pungent muck of some swamp.

On the damp side of the road poison ivy curled over rotting logs and stood silent guard over any possibility of a pistol's tomb. Peter began to feel less tense and reasoned that no one visited here and those that did drove down here quickly on a dare or for a passionate park. His Luger rested safe for a score when the only round in the gun would corrode to the barrel and some industrious insects would loot the powder for some underground excavation.

By now the search and fresh air steeled him and he could see a small building ahead. "I couldn't properly kill myself, maybe curiosity might." Such a lonely looking place bared exploration on foot. A young forest on the right hid behind massive maples with branches that the county plows scared every winter. Among them thrust up a craggy ironwood two feet in diameter that a steel-loaded freight train could not knock over. Eight feet up its trunk protruded a flat piece of metal that had once been nailed to a smaller tree. The paint of this little sign had flaked away and the bark slowly swallowed the letters. Peter read it, "NONG" and raised an eyebrow.

This mystery was short lived for this city boy unaccustomed to the signs of the country. As he approached a garage in the middle of the road he found another "DEAD END" with the same flat, rusted sign bolted below it, "NO HUNTING." The garage crouched like a lion at the mouth of his den covered by a thicket of overgrown cedars and a stone the size of a slain elephant waiting to be devoured. The golden brown asphalt siding was interrupted by two cathedral like windows for eyes and an overhead door for a gaping mouth. More signs adorned the door like blood dripping teeth that warned, "NO TRESSPASSING," "NO SNOWMOBILES," and "BEWARE OF DOG." Peter did not hear any barking, but he began to understand no hunting wove a tight theme here as the garage told him twice more. Finally under the eaves of a low pitched roof a sliver of a rising sun cast up five saffron rays to complete the mane of the beast.

These threats certainly traveled down from the top of the food chain. Peter nearly turned to leave when the final black sign caught his eye. He moved directly in front of it and read the white letters.

!! PILGRIM !!
WHOEVER YOU ARE
FROM WHERE YOU COME
WHAT EVER YOU WANT
COME NOT TO US
GO HOME AND MAKE
SOMEONE ELSE HAPPY
OTTO AND ANNA

The curt dis-invitation made laughter hard to hold back. Peter wished he could tell Rita the same once in a while. Instead he endured each of her side yard talks that usually encroached on his front door, burst into his kitchen before flowing through the living room out to the dock with the kids. Still, just as any excuse attracted her more to meddling in his life he piqued as to the source of such a message. A force pulled his gaze over the two-track that curled under two crab-apples in fragrant full-bloom. "I wonder where this goes," he said before his hackles instantly threw an icy sweat down his spine at the words behind him.

"Shtraight zu Hell!"

Brett Ramseyer

.

4

Peter descended through a blaze of circles. His somber black suit coat bunched up above his shoulder blades as he slid down the coatroom wall of the Goldstein and Heineman Funeral Home. He slumped next to a cache of overcoats that ran the spectrum of their breed, tan, gray, brown and black. The thick metal hangers over his head pinged together every time a new visitor opened one of the double glass doors from outside and let in the February freeze. Some turned into the closet to drop their winter wraps, but invariably decided to hang them over their folded arms for the remainder of their visitation when they saw Peter's head in his hands. They silently turned, but always within ear shot said, "Poor Peter." as if he were an orphan of eight instead of six months shy of his thirty-ninth birthday.

The placard wreathed in white roses near the casket read:

Isaac Gabriel Sonderling
May 12, 1911
To
February 10, 1984

At first Peter stood in the front parlor smiling weakly and wet eyed to the adults of his youth who now stooped below him. He listlessly gazed down at the top of their hoary heads and studied the age spots that lined the widening parts in their hair. The old Jewesses held Peter's elbows to say, "Your vater vas ahh real Mensch." before looking at their spouses who would nod in solemn agreement. He started counting cream colored scarves and black leather gloves to distract himself from the body in the other room.

It only stayed a body until he saw his mother, Claudia, reach into the silver casket to hold Isaac's hand. It seemed an endless pause before something dramatic, Peter's long quick strides behind trenches and topcoats was only half the scene. Claudia forced Peter to slump on the floor and half the visitors to turn their heads and swallow as she bent over her husband to put her lips to that chilly face with its eyes caked shut.

***

Peter whirled from the start of that sudden voice and shuddered dizzyingly from the force of jet eyes overtly preying from a path in the woods. The stare held him in a paralysis of awe saved for celestial miracles or holocaust horror. Those eyes read Peter as easily as the signs behind him and looked through shafts of darkness of which Peter did not yet have the courage to mine.

Brett Ramseyer

"Vhy can't you find anozer place zu die?" awoke Peter from his terrified trance only to send him on another flight of frenzy at what he saw. The pupils and irises blended into one of the most powerful mixes Peter ever saw, but the face in which they were set was gone. A barren landscape of scars that undulated red, brown and white up the throat replaced the face. Tissue stood confused where decades old cicatrix pulled at a wound that could never close. Hills of cells grew up the chin, erased the lips and strained the cheek bones. Pale white mounds rose and suddenly dipped into dark pocks that dispersed under those eyes like a moraine of torment. The rage of flames once stripped this tract of flesh in an instant; a glacier of healing pressed and twisted it for a lifetime.

"I was – looking – a-at the signs," stammered Peter.

"If you vould read inshtead of looking you vould know zu leave."

The simple rudeness of the old man rubbed Peter's tender nerves like pumice. He only heard this grating voice speak a handful of sentences, but just as last night he found a voice of his own to lash out with. "This is a county road isn't it? I didn't cross any fences or trample any flowers."

"Na ja, but old men must be careful, tree steps srough zhe gate und I vould never catch you.

"Well I don't need catching. I will be on my way." Peter started to make brisk strides around the man and his knotted walking stick when a spotted hand seized his shoulder with delicate power.

"Nicht so schnell. Could you help an old man?" Peter could hear the softening of the voice which incensed him more. He furrowed his brow and thought of kicking the cane out from under the old Kraut like the stand from a bike. Peter could see him slowly tipping to the earth with his limbs spinning helplessly like spokes, but the man shuffled through the dust back to the trail from which he had emerged. The distance of only four steps that took what seemed half a minute. Lying hidden in the periwinkle, a garbage bag rattled with cans and clinked with glass. He dared not bend over so he hooked the sack with the crooked end of his cane and pulled it up to his fingers. "Please. Trow zhis avay."

"Where does it go?

"Valk srough zhe gate across zhe road. Follow zhe path shtraight ahead up zhe hill. Zu zhe right of zhe brambles ist a hole. Trow it da. Den ve will discuss vhat you vere looking for."

Peter froze and his anger fell away. He looked into the black eyes that gave away nothing, but he knew. He nodded silently grabbed the bag and walked through the gate.

***

Doreen always interrupted the silence of a Sunday evening when she put her hand on the pine handrail and leaned into the dark basement. "Pete! Garbage." She usually only remembered an hour after dinner when

18

the kids left the house in quiet. Claudia, a budding thirteen-year-old, would be three doors down Linden Ave. in a clandestine middle school meeting of girls. She often met friends in giggling pink bedrooms to discuss the tribulations of surviving a weekend's separation from each other or to plot the overthrow of some competing social regime who just bought newer blouses or cuter shoes. Michael, still two months green with license would scan the refrigerator after dinner for missing items so he could pick up three friends on his way to the grocery store. It would be at least an hour before he returned with a bottle of ketchup and no change left from a five. It left only Peter.

"Hey! Garbage, Pete! It's rotting under the sink." Doreen often saved these shouts for the middle of a fight that had not started yet.

Peter would either roll his eyes from some corner of the basement and spike the business section on the floor or scream "I'm busy." from his office. Either way he would thunder up the stairs after a few more calls to duty. "Where's Michael? Make Claudie do it. What happened to women's liberation?" But the basement lay as silent as the correspondence on the curb stinking of potato peels.

Peter customarily skipped dinner with the family during tax season even on Sunday. He quietly told Michael he would miss it and disappeared. Doreen only shrugged and left his plate on the table after she and Claudia cleared everything. Doreen dismissed it all as some procrastinating clients who turned in their receipts during the first week of April that over-stressed Peter's time. She gave him little thought until she yelled for him. Now she glanced through the rooms and scrunched up her face in contemplation. She quickly filled not with concern, but with frustration. "Where the hell is Peter?"

***

His apprehension about discussing the gun almost made him throw the trash into the hole and lope quickly through the woods down to his Mercedes before the old man could see him leave. He looked through the black tree trunks over the knoll and shuddered at the darkness there. He felt if he did not go back to the man's house, that melted face and searing eyes would haunt him forever.

Peter climbed the hill and down again to find the narrow trail snaking through the periwinkle where the man disappeared. He continued his gait in hopes it made him appear confident instead of revealing his cowardice. He caught the man before he even broke through a row of densely overgrown cedars hiding the small house from the road. His white head turned and waved Peter past into a small opening of neglected lawn alongside a small home covered in cheap asphalt siding. Rusted nail heads showed through a gaudy collection or rectangles that interlocked together in the attempt to appear like brick if the passerby could simply stand the optimum distance from it, but the forest encroached in only to smother Peter too close and make him cringe at the workmanship.

Forcing bravado Peter spoke first, "What a lovely brick home you have."

* * *

The Cheney House skulked low, especially at twilight. The hulking oaks overhead spread out dark arthritic fingers that barely swayed in the spring zephyr to scratch over the hip roof. Course upon course of brick squinted low, perpetually vigilant against interlopers and sitting warily beneath its towering white neighbors. A shin high stack of ledge-stone crossed in front like some ancient fortification that proved unworthy of protecting the family inside. Each owner maintained it out of sentimentality or laziness or helplessness or some tragic flaw. It stood mostly because people more frequently practice the skill of building walls rather than tearing them down. Next to it rose a bastion of brick around a terrace and square pillars stood the sentinels over the concrete walk.

"That's safety," whispered Peter to himself. *No one dare deliver letters here in hopes of luring the Mistress of the house to a lamppost rendezvous.* Peter did not usually look intently at the houses lining the streets in Oak Park when he walked, but tonight was different. He escaped. He took himself out with the trash and followed the curb down Linden, across Chicago, up Land and circled through the avenues of the neighborhood. He passed by Edwin H. Cheney's house many times before in his ambling, but in this evening he saw. The horizontal rings drew him in while the vertical lines of the leaded glass looked like bars on the windows. *The kids are secure. No intruder will steal you away Mrs. Cheney.* But Peter rarely knew the whole story.

* * *

"Vhat ist your shtory?" questioned the German ignoring Peter's levity.

"I'm not sure I have one." He looked into those hypnotic eyes and answered before he could think of a lie. Peter could envision no plot line worth following. In four decades he felt no rising action, no euphoric climax, only changing setting. His answer began to boil his blood again, but his mind flared at the questioner. *You stole my climax and resolution! I finally had something to fill a page.* "You-"

"Nein!" Sharply cut Peter off. "Every ding hat a shtory; for instance, vhat shtory might zhis Luger tell?"

This strange man whose questions singed Peter's cheeks and whose answers charred his nerves pointed to the first concrete step of his porch. There sat the Luger P08 pistol like any harmless garden tool or door stop that had been kicked down the stairs. Peter froze afraid to pick it up. *Come on take it. It's yours.*

Come Not To Us

"Es ist yours. Take it," said the man. "I have no use for do you?"

"Yes, point taken everything has a story. My father told m̲ was the most frightening gun he'd ever known. So – I bought it last year during a rash of break-ins around my neighborhood. Gotta protect the kids."

"I do not doubt zhat your Vater spoke zo, but zhis reason you have given me ist falsch. Vater's teach zhe most memorable lessons. Mein told me:

"Jedes Gesicht spricht treue Gedichte,

Aber niemand schreibt die richtige Geschichte."

"I don't speak German and I don't know you, but *I know* you haven't known me long enough to call me a liar!" fired Peter.

"Ah, sveet anger, I know you vell." mused the man. "Only zhe falsch grow hot vhen zhey are caught. Ja?" he chuckled. "Pick up zhe veapon und shoot vun of us. Zhe suspense ist killing me." Now he laughed outright and Peter sat vanquished on the first step next to the Luger. "Zee, mein Vater shtill lives -- zhe bastard." Peter put his head in his hands and pushed up the wrinkles on his forehead with his outspread fingers. He tried to edit his expression with eight fingertip erasers, but the omission of anger left only emotional emptiness, a blank page of renewed despair.

"Vhat mein Vater said vas zomeding like 'Every face speaks true poetry, but no vun writes down zhe proper shtory.'" Lost again Peter reached for the gun. The black grip chilled his hands white. Each minute in his life felt colder as if he finally reached the bottom of a well. His palm pressed against the square end of the butt and his fingers traced the circle of the trigger guard before he slipped it in his pocket and looked up with his hand outstretched.

"I'm Peter Sonderling and I apologize for disturbing you last night." They shook hands firmly and surprisingly Peter felt himself being pulled to his feet.

"Bitte, no apologies. If you hat not shtopped und sreatened my life I vould haf hat no reason zu remember my ninety-sechs birsday." The ancient hand found the middle of Peter's back and swiveled him toward the pink door. "Come in. Ve'll stain our Kaffee mit Milch."

"I – I couldn't."

"Nonsense, vhat plans could you have? You're supposed zu be dead," and he laughed again. "Call me Otto, Otto Hitzig.

Brett Ramseyer

5

The mouth of Otto's home held the night's chill like a murderer holding his breath before he strikes, all anxiety and excitement, but another element hung thick in the musty entry. It oozed from the pores, slowly. It traced the bridge of an Indian's nose whose profile hung on the wall perpetually staring at the grooves of a heavy pink door. It dripped its cloudy minerals off a rusted iron sculpture of gulls flying over a frog pond's reeds only to collect in columns like jagged stalagmites. It watched Peter's hair blow when Otto opened the door to the hot dry belch of wood heat. It pressed down on Peter with persistence and even plunked down solidly on the built-in-bench to the right to wait out this visitor.

Otto let Peter in and then squeezed the door shut. He pointed down the murky narrow hall to an equally dark room filled with books. "Sit in da," was all he said as he shuffled off to a lighter corner of the house. Peter craned his neck and squinted to see if his eyes could pierce the darkness ahead. His cautious tread followed his hand down the wall groping for a switch. Beneath him the floor rippled with each footfall and moaned with each release. Clinging to life, the house hoped to hug someone into the grave with it, but today Peter almost welcomed its closeness.

Darting around the corners of the passageways careened the echo of clumsily handled pots. Peter sat in an overstuffed, under cleaned chair and began to sway imperceptibly to the syncopated rhythm of shuffling feet moving from cupboard to cupboard interspersed with the whistle of a teapot and the rattle of a spoon in a cup. The sounds of a home somehow managed to penetrate this cave and lull Peter to sleep.

When he awoke his eyes adjusted to see well enough in the darkness as all eyes tend to do. The brown window panes allowed enough light to pass to send a faint glint off the golden spines of the books ringing the room. Their red and black covers dulled under a frost of dust.

The end of a sound woke Peter up. The steady rasp of a finished record screeched still as Otto snatched the needle up and placed it on the rest arm. Otto stooped over a small table fumbling for an elusive clinking chain before he pulled it and cast a single bulb's glow around the room from under a green glass lampshade. Peter recoiled at the pain the light brought after his time in the dark. He held up his hand suddenly and tried to peek through his fingers.

"How long have I been asleep?"

"A lifetime – zhe Kaffee ist kuhl und zhe record has finished."

"I didn't even hear you put on a record. What do you listen to out here?"

"Out here? Dis ist not zhe edge of zhe earth. It ist zhe center of zhe universe because ve are here und zhe spieler lifts up our souls from zhe muck." Otto took a white dust jacket off of a corner shelf and shuffled back over to the small record player. He slipped the forty-five over the thick post capped in red. He set the needle heavily down and began to speak over the pulsing sibilance of the needle dragging through the grooves. "I listen to zhe Meisters, today – Beethhoven." And a piano's sudden base chord pounced from the small black box and shook Peter. As it died away, treble paws tread cautiously over the staff until their hurried pace grew into an emotional chase of happiness, disappointment and fear. The hunt surged and slowed before one last race left the stalker empty as if a mouse had slipped away through a crack in the wall. Peter could not identify his mood after hearing the sounds of escape. He sat silently split between remorse and relief.

"What was that piece?"

"It vas zhe first movement of Beethoven's Pathetique Sonata. Zhe second section vill probably be more familiar zu you." Its mellowness softly washed over Peter's anxiety and he commiserated in a stranger's lamp lit room with the waves of sound.

When the Adagio cantabile struck its last key Peter opened his eyes and sipped his coffee cut slightly sweet with sugar and cream. He kept the small saucer and cup near his mouth to cover the silence between the two men that the now quickening music could not fill and to remind him not to stare at the old man's scars. If the lower half of his face actually sagged from his cheeks Otto would have seemed more real, but it pulled tightly over the corners of his jaw merely as an outline of his skeleton. Even at ninety-six his chest filled perpetually with an enormous drive that appeared as if it could still rouse an army. Otto's presence made small talk a ridiculous notion which piqued Peter through cycles of revulsion and attraction that coincided with the rise and fall of the old man's lungs.

"You say yesterday was your birthday?"

"Ja."

"April 20th. New moon last night, I can't remember a time when it was so dark. I couldn't see you when you interrupted my-"

"Failed attempt."

"Yeah- I'm sorry if I frightened you or woke you up."

"Nonsense, I shleep little und haven't felt fear zince my first vife died. How ist your vife?"

"At home with the kids in Chicago, probably."

"I said, 'How,' nicht vhere your vife ist. You are alvays evading qvestions. If you mean to hide zomeding, place it in zhe open mit such

24

volume zhat no vun vill bozher to remember it all. Den it ist zo easy zu say 'I told you zo' und zhe fault lies mit zhe ozher person. Don't be lazy mit zhe details und don't leave zhe details for somevun else to supply or Gott forbid figure out for you. Na ja, ve'll shtart again. Vhere in Chicago?"

"Oak Park."

"Ah, zhe birsplace of Hemingway, zhe seat of Frank Lloyd Wright's genius und philandering und zhe home to zhe vealth of Chicago's stagnant middle class."

New surprise dialated Peter's eyes only to make him squint it away with suspicion. "How do you know all that?"

"I'm an old man who lives alone in zhe voods. Zhose Buchs around our heads aren't decorations to impress zhe neighbors. In fact I vas reading vhen you parked your car last night." A tinge of malevolence accompanied his chuckle, "I sought ein Paar of local teenagers overcome mit zhe early flow of shpring vere here to tap a tree, zo to speak. I usually am zhe only vun who does any tapping, on zheir foggy vindows mit my cane. Zhe American teenager can go from absolute nah-ked to sixty in under five seconds." Even Peter could not help himself from laughing at a vision of the harmless fear of a sixteen-year-old with his jeans knotted around his ankles, blood draining from some veins and thumping through others as he careened down this dirt road to safety.

Otto wiped his leaking right eye in mirth and became more solemn in tone. "Imagine my surprise to zee a confused man illuminated by his own headlamps mit a Luger at his temple."

"That wasn't confusion – it was conviction, Mr. Hitzig."

"Bitte, call me Otto und excuse me, it vas confusion. Even zhe children have enough sense to turn out zhe lights."

"I had a plan of how I wanted myself to die. I wanted lights!" flailed Peter.

"Conviction carries out a plan und conviction uses a Walther not a Luger."

"What?"

"Your Luger ist an inferior veapon, magnificent craftsmanship, but inferior. Zhey vere all replaced in 1938 by zhe Walther P38. Now zhat vas a veapon. It seems zhat pistol vould have put more fear in your Vater. I have myself seen an officer pull out a Luger at close range zu kill a prisoner vhen zhe mechanism jammed mit dirt und inshtead of a qvick shot to zhe skull he exhausted himself pistol vhipping zhe prisoner. It vas embarrassing, a German should rise above such flailing displays, und design a pistol zhat verks – zhe Walther never jammed."

Peter did not know whether to be appalled by the story or interested in a first hand account of such callous violence. The callousness of the officer did not make him cringe, but that of Otto, because he did not even blink at the memory of cold murder. The death shined only as a sidelight to the gun and the old German's sympathy did not illuminate the victim. The old man's disgust weighed not with the officer's actions, but that he spent time working up a sweat to dispense with the prisoner. Peter sat there in a new world that he thought and hoped lay extinct some forty years before, but he leaned in to know more.

"Why did the officer kill the man?"

"I know not. It vas a Fraulein – she vas a stinking Jew, who had led him astray." Peter's guts began to twist around the words 'Stinking Jew.' He pressed in for her sake wanting to hear her story so he might quell the swell of solitary torture she endured. Avenging her death felt almost possible, just with knowing. "What was her name?" he whispered without knowing he had spoken.

Otto's obvious disgust carved deepening creases in his high forehead as he expected to ask questions. "I didn't know den und I can't be expected zu remember such an insignificant detail forty years after."

"I thought we weren't supposed to be lazy with details," said Peter finally feeling like he was gaining the upper hand. "So how does a German World War II veteran take up residence in Michigan?"

"Who says I vas in Verld Vor II?" Otto shot back.

"Well, a German officer pistol whipping nameless Jews sounds awfully Nazified if you ask me."

"Nein. I asked you not. I left Germany after Verld Vor I. Vhat I did ask you vas, how ist your vife, und you have tried zu cloud zhe entire conversation mit nonsense. She ist vhy you came zu zhe end of my road, ist she not?"

Peter paused while the vision of Rita Van Duinnen peeking around white lace curtains rose in his mind, but then he looked at Otto's hard lips and twisted face. "Why are you interested?"

"I zee zo few people any more. I feel like a soldier's tattered limb zhat hast been severed und cast avay zu rot. Zhere ist zo little feeling. Let an old man live srough your pain." And his black eyes softened in a convincing way.

Ninety-six. He could drop dead before you even finish the story. Let it out -- "I don't know how Doreen is anymore."

"Doreen?"

"My wife – we don't talk anymore. We yell. The funny thing is the louder we shout the less we listen. At least I don't listen much when she-" caught in Peter's throat as painfully honest statements can. He tried to clear it away with a grunt and a sip of coffee.

"Marriage. Silence falls and zo does the Kratzer." Otto's right eye began to merrily ooze again.

Peter's left eyebrow rose in misunderstanding. "'Kratzer?'"

Come Not To Us

"Ja, Kratzer. Somevun has been scratching your vife's itch."

I just said we've been fighting! You don't have any idea what you're talking about and it's our eighteenth anniversary next month all came rushing up Peter's throat, but crashed into his soft palate like bile filled nausea.

***

Peter's groomsmen stood around him laughing hysterically and the North Broadway traffic honked noisily by without sympathy. Peter's bloodshot eyes still bulged grotesquely with his last heave into the storm drain. He wiped his mouth on the back of his hand as he wearily sat on the curb. His one AM whiskers suspended like blunt needles in his face that registered each bump with a wince in his otherwise numb skin.

A steady May drizzle drove the oil out of the street and reflected a verdant sheen from the curling neon sign of the Green Mill overhead. To the eyes of the inebriate an emerald smear blurred underneath the cars, caught wings on the mist spun from tires and descended quietly on the foliage of St. Boniface Cemetery down the block.

"I wanna be dead." moaned Peter with his eyes now closed before his stomach stormed again in the drain.

"Naw," said a cousin slapping Peter on the shoulder. "Ten shots won't kill ya, ya pantywaist."

"Suck it up, Pete."

"Let's go, man."

"I can't, you pukes," croaked Peter.

"Look who's talking,'" offered some other cousin Peter did not like from the edge of the circle. Everyone laughed. "Now's the time for our old family tradition, Pete." Peter looked up to see it was his cousin Wendell standing six foot three. The kink in his coarse brown hair stood frozen in a slush of hair oil. His glance always raced between the corners of his eyes in a perpetual infatuation with what lay around a corner.

Peter always hated Wendell's traditions. Wendell's birthday, July 19th, a day before Peter's was an easy day to remember. The only day of the year that Wendell shared the same age with Peter accompanied the only voluntary visit Wendell paid his cousin, usually to brag. The day they were both ten Peter saw Wendell furiously peddling a glistening red bike down the sidewalk. Wendell proceeded to gush over every reflector and spoke, his top speed, and ability to slide to a stop. The next day Peter's hopes of a better bike met with a pair of used black roller skates. He hated Wendell.

"We don't want our family marrying if it isn't meant to be. Now Doreen may be one of the tastiest looking dishes I've ever seen, but we wouldn't want an ugly divorce. Right fellas? So the Witz branch of the family has created a little test. You've already passed the first part; you're drunk. The second is a bit tougher. We call it, 'Find the Altar.'" Suddenly

27

Wendell and all Peter's other cousins raced down to Lawrence Avenue to hop on the Red Line.

Before the group rounded the corner out of sight Peter tried to stand and follow, but slipped in a puddle of his own dizziness and sick. "Bastards! I can't walk! What the-" His hand reached out to steady himself on the wet concrete and finally to sit. "Great, I'm gonna get mugged Uptown." While Peter tried to blink away the blur a man separated from the shadows in a white fedora with a black band and red feather. His syncopated strut drew Peter's attention with its rhythmic exaggeration. It was an unflappable cadence that even the bass line leaking through the walls of the jazz club could not alter. He stopped over Peter with one leg down in the street.

"Yeah, you gentlemen in the mood for love tonight?" He pulled a small brass key connected to a black diamond shaped keychain from the breast pocket of his tightly tailored suit coat. "Here's the key to ecstasy. No need for luck, just five sawbucks and I'll find you a-"

"No thanks," came from behind Peter. "Come on," and he was lifted by his armpit to his feet and swung to the door. "I say we go back into the Mill for more music." Tony Sciori's grip propped up his friend.

"Hey man, suit yourself. No dent in my wealth, if you put your dick on a shelf..."

"Thanks for the poetry," yapped Tony over Peter's shoulder as he held open the door with his foot. Smoke and stale beer wafted out as did the rustle of a few early morning patrons shuffling to the bathroom to return their leased Schlitz to the urinals while the band milled between sets. Tony lugged Peter over to the end bar where he set a stool under him like a tripod, balanced him carefully before he walked down to the bartender and sloshed back with two fizzing rocks glasses. He took one and slid it skillfully down the bar where it stopped with a light clink against Peter's temple. He sat up with a ring of condensation dripping into his eyes left from someone's cold mug.

"Thanks."

"Don't mention it. It's just soda. I pointed at you and the bartender just filled the glasses, no charge."

"No, I mean for staying with me. I thought everybody was on the El."

"Well, this just proves what they say. It's a good thing you can pick your friends because you're stuck with your family.

"Yeah, well Wendell's always been a prick. He'll be sad he missed the pimp though. God, this neighborhood has gone to shit. Sinatra sang here a few years ago."

"The music's still good. Just don't sit outside drunk, inviting trouble."

28

Come Not To Us

"Doreen will kill me if I show up late tomorrow."

"Relax. I'm here. It's not even two in the morning and you don't have to be at the church until noon."

"Synagogue."

"Whatever. You're lucky no matter where it is. What I wouldn't give for a girl like-"

"Easy!"

"Hey be nice. You need me to get home tonight. I have half a mind to kick you into an alley and show up in your tux tomorrow, but I will uphold my duties as best man to ensure your lady is happy and lands next to you at the end of the runway tomorrow."

"Should I show gratitude or punch you?"

"Gratitude. You're still too drunk to fight. Hey, quick the Capone booth just opened up let's slide in and listen awhile." Tony led the way for Peter moving chairs and warning the full ones. "Drunk man walkin' here! Drunk man walkin'!"

Peter slid across the gold velvet cushions of the booth. "Normally that would have embarrassed me, but not tonight. Tonight I'm too drunk and tomorrow – tomorrow I marry. Even you, Tony, can't ruin my confidence."

A young slender black woman stepped to the bandstand and began adjusting the microphone stand. The bass player and the drummer walked in from the back where they had been smoking something. One anxiously tightened strings, plucked short chromatic growls only to loosen them back where he began while the other stirred the brushes over the head of a snare washing the room in the sound of the rain.

"I'm confident too, Pete, and in love."

"Oh yeah, who's the woman this week?"

Tony nodded toward the bandstand. "Would you look at the tits on her." The singers black dress fit tightly on her straight frame and Peter frowned.

"I don't see any. Since when are you into black women?"

"No, it's milky white tonight, in the corner. Just what I need, a great body, plenty to eat, likes jazz clubs and doesn't talk too much." Then Peter laughed with Tony over the fruit bedecked maiden glistening green from the Green Mill neon blaring from the wall.

"I need more than a statue."

"You've got more than that."

"I know."

"Are you ready for the plunge?"

"I told you. I'm confident. I'm ready."

"This is the Capone booth you know. It's a lot like marriage."

"Oh, here you go. I can't wait for this, wax philosophical for me."

Brett Ramseyer

"Hold your breath lover boy we're goin' to the bottom of the river on this one."

"I'm already at the bottom, I'm drunk remember. How 'bout you bring me back up before I drown in it."

"Do you know why this is the Capone booth? Huh?"

"Because it's shaped like a C?"

"You know what, just shut up and listen. You might learn something. Look there you see the front door?" Peter nodded. "And there, the side door?"

"I get it Capone liked doors."

"Pete! You're not funny when you're sober. You're an idiot in a stupor, but you're damn right he liked doors. You know why?" Peter raised his eyebrows as he leaned in over the table. "I'll tell you why. He always had to see every entrance. No sneak raids or attacks. There's never a moment to sit confident and unaware in the mob."

"So, the marriage in this story?-"

"Simple. You're joining the biggest mob in America – the married middle class, the status quo."

"I get it. Mob – crime – caught – go to prison. This is too much cliché even for you, Tony. Doreen will not be my ball and chain."

"Please, a little credit. I'm in law school now. I do think about things now. It isn't like undergrad days at U of C. Take Capone, he was in the middle always with an eye out the front door for the law or the side door for the thugs who wanted what he had. So, here he sat in this corner thinking he had the world by the balls when really he was the one in the twist."

"Now, middle class marriage is exactly the same in so many ways I can't even tell you. Hell, the place closes at four. The economics of it all could keep me goin' 'til noon, but I'm talkin' 'bout one kind of problem that comes with marriage. It's the problem of the two doors."

Suddenly, lightly struck piano keys began descending the staff. The piano player finally returned from the bathroom and turned the heads of all the patrons. The thin woman slid to the microphone. Her speaking voice calmed the crowd like a beekeepers cool smoke, and the buzz turned to polite applause. "Good morning everybody, we're back. Thanks for staying up with us. I thought we'd reward you with a little mellow Billie. This is for those of you who have a shoulder to put your head on and maybe you could whisper *These Foolish Things*," and the bass picked up behind her.

Tony leaned toward Peter and spoke in low tones and said, "I love this stuff," while he clapped. "Two doors my friend, that's going to be your new problem. See you'll be sittin' in this booth every day. Doreen will be right here with you. If you're smart you'll keep an eye to both doors because in the front will stream all the women you could have had if Doreen wasn't sittin' right next to you. You'll be kicking yourself for joining the mob and being trapped over here in this corner. Then one day you'll get sloppy. You'll be so mad you went organized that you'll burn over black with rage. Or a song will touch you more than your wife has in months. Or you'll be so damn bored you'll get distracted by that pair of nipples on the statue. Then it happens."

"What happens?"

"You're lost Pete. I already told you your new problem and you've forgotten the second of two parts, the side door. Whenever you screw up, and you will, that door will open. Then quiet as cotton she'll be gone, out into the alley and then up against a brick wall somewhere sweating out the passion that you couldn't give her."

"Tony, you're the worst best man ever."

"As your legal council I advise you not to shoot the messenger."

"I am part of the mob. I've got a sawed-off shotgun under the table."

"Don't worry. I've already talked to Doreen. She told me about how sawed-off you were."

Peter cracked a grin as he slugged Tony in the shoulder before he scooched out of the booth. "Come on. I can stand. Let's get out of here so I can make it to my gang initiation tomorrow."

"Okay, but don't say I didn't warn you."

"Warned," nodded Peter as he weaved a little less precariously through the tables and chairs toward door. "Let's say we go out the front. I'm still a law abiding citizen." They stopped while Peter held the door open with his foot and looked out at the drizzle that had become a deluge. He pulled his collar up around his neck and started a sprint to the El. The music followed them out into the street while the door slowly pulled itself shut.

You came

You saw

You conquered me

When you did that to me

I knew somehow this had to be...

Brett Ramseyer

6

Five hours. The tension rose up Peter's forearms into his neck. He nosed his Mercedes into a passing lane of the Eisenhower Expressway and sped on toward sunset. He tilted his head from left to right and rolled his shoulders over his chest just to hear his spine pop. He craned right for a moment to watch his exit slide by through the passenger window. Instead, a mile and half past Austin he headed north on Harlem to Schneider Avenue.

It's not so close to Linden that Mom can be walking over regularly, but not so far that I should feel guilty for not letting her move in with Doreen and the kids. Well she isn't incapacitated. Dad just – "Hey Ma," Peter called across the street before he rolled to a stop under a sturdy oak still waiting to completely unfurl its spring canopy.

Claudia cut chunks of sod from a derelict rose bed off her front walk. She shook them vigorously to release a shower of dark soil before tossing roots and blades into an awaiting wheelbarrow. She gardened rump to the road and Peter chuckled as he sauntered up the walk with his hands in his front pants pockets. "You know, I woke up to a view pretty much like this in Pentwater this morning."

Mrs. Sonderling, thin like the handles of her gardening tools had worn out useless weight three lives ago. "Baby Speck," she called it, but Peter had never seen those pictures. None of the relics of her first existence survived. She never mentioned the time of burning. At dinner parties she would answer, "I awoke the day Isaac found me," when new acquaintances asked about her past. Isaac would call across the room, "Mein Dornröschen! My briar rose. Seine Blume ist immer so schön daß vergiß ich seine dornliche Zunge." Their German company would chuckle at the fairytale and might launch into a discussion of the brothers Grimm, while the rest would ask for a translation. Isaac would always mention the beautiful blume, but leave out the thorny tongue just to hear her call back to her "Older handsome prince." And with all that the conversation would trip merrily and inconsequentially along.

Now, Claudia straightened at the familiar voice, but did not turn to face him. She thought for a second and bent down back to work before she spoke. She tended to her work under a tight skull cap of white hair pulled back in a bun. "We don't want any here. You can peddle your wares down the street, unless of course you can lend an old woman an ear and I'll tell you about my good for nothing son who promised to edge this bed three weeks ago."

Peter bent down and kissed her on the cheek before he sunk in a spade. "This was half frozen three weeks ago, besides it's tax season Mom. Most of my life revolves around the last three weeks."

"Well, we know it doesn't revolve around your mother."

"Patience is a virtue."

"Tell me, how virtuous is it to lock up your mother in this lonely prison?"

"Damn it! Ma."

"Hold your tongue. Do you want the neighbors to hear," said Claudia letting her eyes dart back and forth at no one.

"You don't even know your neighbors. What d'you care? God, I wonder why I haven't been over here?"

"Remember what I told you when you were young. Sarcasm will get you no where."

"I've been there and back. I think I can take care of myself."

"But not your mother."

"You are bat shit insane! You know that, mother?"

"Peter! The neighbors!" Claudia finally dropped the sod that had been busying her hands. She looked left, but saw only the husk of her son rubbing his temples with his palm across his eyes. She turned, full in the face, hoping she would see some glimmer of her husband alive in Peter, but he only leaned down to rest his head on the back of his hands propped up by the shovel.

Claudia saw the faint black streak he had smeared on the side of his head and she softened as mothers do when they intended to hold a hard line with their children. They move carelessly toward the edge of a cliff, hopping and dancing up and down before they suddenly look over the edge to a vision of evisceration and ugliness on jagged points below. This time Claudia felt old and too frail to backpedal into a toyshop or soda stand as she might have done in Peter's childhood when she scared herself with her own deformity. Instead she hovered on the precipice trying not to look down. "The neighbors are not strangers. That one there-"

"The red ranch? Asked Peter.

"Yes. It's a family of Polacks. Those are Russians, and" she nodded across the street. "There is a whole row of English." Then her fist flailed down with each word like a doctor trying to resuscitate the dead, "Catholics, Orthodox, Presbyterians, Anglicans," before she came down across her own heart, "and me, the Jew."

Claudia turned away unable to look again at her son, "Schneider is one of the streets writers muse about when they feel the crock pot is starting to melt. Well, it's all a crock Peter. It's nineteen eighty-five; they told me their names and I only remember the labels. I escaped the furnace forty years ago. I have no intention of melting."

Come Not To Us

Claudia allotted herself one tear that hung in the corner of her eye threatening to topple her over the edge and Peter looked up too late to see her blink it off. It alone tumbled down toward the ugliness and left her quite upright on the other side of the chasm that separated her from her son.

***

The Mercedes slipped rather noiselessly past the uncut grass that Michael neglected and into the garage. Only just a few years ago little Claudie in pigtails or Michael with purple popsicle dribbling down his chin would bound out the front door on the mere chance that Dad drove the black car passing down Linden Street, but teenagers are forbidden to feel excitement toward anything remotely related to their parents. Not even a curtain waved in a window when Peter yanked the lawnmower alive in to a sputtering cloud of blue smoke. Only a few passes remained when Michael startled Peter by shouting from behind him, "I was just coming out to do that!"

"Well your timing is impeccable," Peter groused over the drone of the engine. "I'll finish it. You bag the last of the clippings and take them to the curb."

"Aw, Dad. That's Claudie's job."

"And I'm doing yours. Get the bags!" In a final lap Peter finished and Michael had the bags. Before Peter could slide the mower out of the way of the car in the garage Michael bounded back from the street.

"All finished, Dad."

"Not bad for thirty seconds' work. So where were you when I started the mower?"

"Oh yeah, I was in the basement doing my homework on your desk. I didn't hear it start up. Besides, I have an algebra test tomorrow and I figured you wouldn't want me to come out and help until I was fully prepared."

"Uh-huh. How'd you know I was home?"

"I heard – uh – what'd you say?"

"You said you had to finish before you would come out and help and that you didn't hear the mower."

"Well, well the algebra test part is true."

"Busted. Where's your mother?"

"I don't know. She shouted something down to me before she left. She was going to pick up Claudie from somewhere."

"You know your general concern for the well being of your family is really astounding."

"I'll remember that the next time you send me over to Grandma's because you don't want to go."

"Hey! Shut up. You know I've been busy."

"I know. I've hardly seen you lately. I wanted to go to the cottage with you this weekend."

"You didn't tell me."

"Mom told me to let you go alone so you could relax after tax season."

"She was right. I wasn't fit to be with man nor beast this weekend."

"Can I go next time?"

"We'll see. You might have another algebra test," Peter grinned.

"Only if you're going up to clean the gutters or something."

"Speaking of something, your Grandma's expecting you to help her clean out her front rose bed this week."

***

Peter lay under the sheets staring up at the ceiling while a bluish glow of the street lamps seeped around the window shades. He and Doreen spent another night managing to finish their chores in separate rooms. They did not speak even as much as a "How was your trip?" and he knew he would feign sleep when she would lie next to him.

This inner tension drove him north before. He lay dreading the time she would silently slip under the covers and warm her pillow with the fresh scents of lavender or lilies from her Sunday bath. It would drift to his nostrils and awaken a longing revulsion in him that kept him awake and knotted his stomach. He would lay tense in apprehension until assured she slept. *Will she touch me? Will her hand brush my thigh or arm, lay across my chest with soft lovely pressure?*

These things he wanted, to be wrapped in Doreen's aroma of amour once again. Her touch would raise his blood, but it swelled in new colors now. The simple thought made him shut his eyes to blackness until his lids disappeared in wrinkles so tight that he could feel his own pulse trying to push them open with each scarlet jet.

I remember when she looked all pink and turquoise.

***

Doreen's silk scarf streamed behind her neck and waved against a backdrop of Florida Bay that began to lose itself in the vastness of the Gulf. Peter could not stop looking across the narrow body of the roadster at the new Mrs. Sonderling. The white knuckle ride for her traversed across Highway 1 to Whitehead Street because Peter more than once faded toward her guardrail in his looks of stunned admiration. She smiled about it at Sunset Point. She tolerated it over Long Key as Peter's hand began sliding up her skirted thigh. She squealed in fright by Ramrod Key where Peter's luck ran out. He clipped the rearview mirror on the rail, over compensated across the center line, and came to rest in front of an irate delivery truck that stood nearly on its nose. They sat in silence the rest of the drive to Key West, neither glancing over the stick shift again.

Come Not To Us

Minutes after noon they went their separate ways in anger and shame. On her way out the door Doreen said, "I'm going exploring," before Peter bounced their suitcases on their bed at the inn. He struggled to untangle his arms from shoulder straps and Samsonite. She was gone.

At first he tried to find her fuchsia scarf among the shops of Duval Street, but abandoned the chase early with so many tropical colors in a press under the green canopy of palms. Instead he went alone to the Hemingway House farther south. Peter mused momentarily in the writing studio. The tour guide droned on in an incessant wash like the sea over sand. Never being of a literary mind Peter tuned out the informative sibilance only hearing the familiar *"The Sun Also Rises"* and *"The Old Man and the Sea."*

Outside he paid more attention by the immense pool surrounded by green when the tour guide said, "Sir, it's your lucky day. It's a penny. Pick it up." Peter half bent down before he heard the snickers and backed up a bit red-faced. "Just kidding, sir. You're not the first I've fooled. Don't feel bad. You see ladies and gentlemen. It's under glass. The story is a good one like so many here at the house. This sixty-five foot pool was the first built on Key West. In fact it still is the largest pool even now in 1967."

Peter heckled from the back of the gathering now. "A big pool, fascinating!"

"Actually it is, sir. Bear with me. 'Papa' Hemingway drew up the plans for the pool himself, but was away as a correspondent during the Spanish Civil War in '38 and '39. His second wife Pauline was left to supervise the construction and upon completion it came in at around $20,000, a king's ransom at the time. 'Papa' came home, saw the pool and joked with Pauline. He pulled a penny from his pocket and said, 'Well, you might as well take my last cent.' He then took the penny and pressed it into the wet cement of the patio." The group chuckled, quite amused and Peter could feel them give him a sideways glance as if to remind him to be quiet when the tour guide spoke.

He spent the rest of the tour walking through the grounds trying to look interested in polydactyl cats, but six toes or not, he could not help thinking that 'Papa's' house in paradise had become little more than a litter box for strays. It somehow disgusted him with a layer of sadness. *God, a guy gets famous, important even. He dies and in less than a decade Tom and Sylvester walk around pissing on everything like they own the place. No wonder he killed himself. Who could live in a world like this?*

His mood shifted to worry as he lay face up in the honeymoon suite watching the blades of the ceiling fan indolently spinning. The clock nearly struck four when Doreen returned as abruptly as she escaped. Her hands waved over the bed like tulle in and island breeze only it was tissue paper from artist galleries and tchotchkie shops. Doreen bubbled over with what she saw and what they should revisit tomorrow. She smiled sappily over

what she bought and how Peter should like it as much as she. "Won't
Sunset over Fort Taylor look nice on our bedroom wall when we have one?"

"Yes, Dear," and Peter began to reach a new understanding with
Ernest Hemingway. He smiled. "It's a nice water color, Doreen. How
'bout the bathroom?" His unappreciated joke was met with pursed lips and
a raised eyebrow. Peter just held the painting in front of him with his arms
stretched wider than his smile and he nodded, while she unwrapped more
precious things and laid them across the bed spread. "My last cent."

"What's that sweetie?"

"Oh nothing. Say, you have to come with me to Hemingway's
House tomorrow. He's got a great pool."

"Shut up and kiss me. We're on our honeymoon."

***

She's always been like that Peter thought still lying in bed with
dread-desire. *Never an explanation. Never an apology. She's not different.
It's been eighteen years. Only the colors have changed.*

The light from over the sink left the room and Doreen entered.
She slid silently between the white sheets and did not cause a ripple on the
mattress. She rolled on her side to face the wall and Peter lay relieved in his
disappointment that ferried him off to sleep.

7

The groggy rush of Monday morning saw the family mechanically preparing themselves for the start of a new spring week. Golden juice sloshed over the countertops without a cloth to wipe it up. Black crumbs clung to the sides and bottom of the kitchen sink scraped clean from a piece of smoldering toast that made the entire house smell of cheap coffee grounds. Only the scents hung in the air by the time Peter willed himself from under the covers. He lay awake before Doreen's alarm sounded and filled in the actions of his children as he heard the knocking, yelling and bumbling of their routine. He waited through half an hour of silence before he started his own sounds.

Peter walked down the hall scratching under his white boxer shorts. Three chosen and discarded outfits crept out of Claudie's bedroom all some variant of pink and he tried not to think of his wife. On the kitchen table leaned Michael's sack lunch. Forgotten and stretching for the garage it begged to be snatched up and eaten at a crowded cafeteria table. Instead Peter sat down heavily and crinkled into the brown bag to mysteriously find only an apple and some carrot sticks. He resigned himself to the healthy start and munched horse-jawed and mindlessly until only his fingers lay in the bag.

Eating Michael's lunch reminded him of their conversation. "The general well being of your family" stuck in his craw like a mouthful of chalk. Doreen dropped the kids at school on her way to work and left a lonely house. There was only one place for Peter to go if "the well being" was to matter.

The walk really was no more than a mile and a quarter to Schneider Ave. He took three steps up the walk past the rose bed that still suffered from neglect. He turned around the unassuming brick one story to the unlocked shed in the side yard. He found the rusted wheelbarrow, a flat spade and hand cultivator and set to work without announcing his presence. Still, he saw a fragile lace curtain flutter in the sitting room before he even lifted the first clump of overgrowth. He knew she would watch him the entire time so he stopped looking up. He thought he would leave her with her illusion of stealth.

When he finished he rasped his hands together to rub loose the dirt and looked down at his sodden knees. Quickly the wheelbarrow leaned against a wall and the spade and cultivator hung in their proper places. He slid from the shed to face his mother leaning out the back door off the kitchen. "Come in to clean up. I've got coffee ready."

Brett Ramseyer

Peter followed the orange path in the brown linoleum that had appeared over the decades. It made sharp square turns in the middle of the kitchen apparently around the edge of some giant dining table no longer there. The path stopped dead at the sink where Peter bent to wash up to his elbows. It made a broad swath between the refrigerator and stove where he dried himself on a nearly thread bare towel. He looked at the once cream colored walls that now stood gray with years of cooking and no cleaning. The room had all the utilitarian appeal of a jail cell and even less decoration.

The bare walls held only a small calendar that hung next to a beige phone whose cord dangled four feet in a spiral to the floor. It was an old calendar, from last year. It stood on February with exes crossing corner to corner through the first nine boxes of the month. The picture, a frozen scene, portrayed a stretching maple tree that traced a black web above a stark snowscape. A silver sheen hung on the limbs from an overnight ice storm and a solitary cardinal perched on one of the lower limbs stared hungrily over a desolate field of corn stubble.

Claudia sat at a small round table well within the confines of the orange rectangle pouring cream into the coffee. Peter sat across from her as she sprinkled a spoonful of sugar into each cup. She stirred each once without touching the sides then slid saucer and all across to her son. "Fortunate is the mother to have such a son."

"That wasn't the story I heard yesterday."

"Well every day has its own tale. What is yours today? It's Monday. I thought you would be working."

"I am mother, one rose bed, complete."

"You know what I mean. You're still an accountant aren't you? All your clients haven't left you have they?"

"No, no. It is the nature of it for me since I've moved out on my own. April is the month with two halves not March. It's frenzy and flotsam, but never out of order."

"Taxes?"

"Yes."

Claudia nodded and sipped. "So what does the rest of the cruelest month hold for you?"

"Down time. At least for this week."

"Tax season is a year away. How does an accountant keep himself counting?"

"I keep the books for several small businesses in the area. It keeps me pretty near full time and if I want more I start soliciting shops downtown."

"Like Doreen's flower shop?"

"Yes, except that's like putting money from my left pocket into my right. It just saves us having to pay someone else to keep track. It frees

Come Not To Us

Doreen to be more creative in finding new business and arranging. She's doing really well," said Peter as he became more keen on his coffee cup than looking into his mother's eyes. "She cleared a profit for the first time last year and paid down the store in January."

"How are you doing, Peter?"

"I've kept us out of the poor house and put you in a new one."

"You know that's not what I meant."

"I know."

"I – I haven't seen you much lately. I guess it boiled over yesterday."

"No, I deserved that, Mother."

"Probably, but a mother is supposed to sense these things with her children especially now that your father is gone. Who else do I have to think about? That's part of the problem. I have a lot of long hours to stew over why you haven't visited. It's not fair of me. You're in the middle of your life: kids, work, wife and here I am at the end. I know you're busy."

"Still, I should get over to the house more."

"Well, here you are and the house is one of those things we need to talk about."

"I know. You hate it."

"No, I wouldn't say that exactly. I want to throw some business your way."

"Another left to right pocket deal?"

"Not at all, my money is as green as the next person's."

"You're not thinking of paying me for the rose bed are you? I'm paying the note on this place. It really isn't your expense. Do you want to spruce up some of these rooms because I will do it or hire someone to do the work. You shouldn't have to pay for improving my property."

"I'm not thinking home improvement, Peter. It's more like a long over due paperwork spring cleaning. Follow me." The two followed the orange path through the casement to the sitting room. She led him down the short hallway where she pulled a dangling string that ignited a bare forty watt bulb. It cast a brown glow on the last door that Claudia fumbled to open with an equally brown skeleton key that hung under clothes and around her neck.

Peter raised a quizzical eyebrow and smiled. "What kind of war secrets you hiding back here, Mother? You live alone for God's sake. Even a thief would take one look at the naked walls of this place and leave thinking it was abandoned. There can't be too much of a security risk."

Claudia's focus darted guiltily from Peter and she pushed the door open. It creaked so loudly that it sounded more like a staccato series of cracks before it hit with a thud on one of dozens of cardboard boxes stacked around the room. "You don't know that much about your father and me."

"What do you mean?"

"I've had such a difficult time since Isaac died."

"I know. That's why we moved you out of the old house with so many memories and to be nearer to us."

"I didn't need you to buy this house for me."

"Of course not, not entirely. You had the money from the sale."

"There's more."

"More where?"

"Many places."

"How come I don't know about these things?"

"Oh Peter, what parent tells their child everything?"

"But you haven't told me anything. How many places?"

"Dozens. What can I say? We're war survivors. We've hidden things, stashed them away for fiery days. Sometimes I think we did it without thinking because it is how we lived. In the camps I hid everything, scraps of food, bandages. We even tried to hide our fear in our pillows. I had a small red pouch once. It used to be red, but it blackened soon enough. I'd tie it with bits of gauze I would steal from the hospital barracks. I was given two hard candies once. I hid those and one saved me, I think. I wrapped them carefully in my pouch when the staff wasn't looking and spirited them away between my legs. I didn't tell the guard who was about to beat me where I had been hiding them. He just held it between his teeth and sucked on the sugar. The other eased me off to sleep that night."

Peter stood with his jaw slack and slightly quivering. Forty years had not elicited a single morsel of her war life, not a gristled scrap, nor a dry crumb and this morning sweets. It was far too sticky, like a mouth full of caramel after a month's fast. He could not swallow or chew. He could barely breathe around it and it made his eyes water. He could not ask about what she hid then or what she hid now. He could only stand and wait.

Claudia broke the candied jaws of mother and son whose wide-eyed stance started to turn them away from each other. "I think the money is mostly locked into insurance policies; but there are investments. To tell the truth I don't know the particulars. Isaac handled our books. He could hide things even without meaning to."

"I don't know what to say. This is –"

"– A lot to hear. This is the business I need you to do. If you can," said Claudia as she knelt carefully on the floor and pulled two cardboard boxes filled with files toward her. "These are all Isaac's papers. I haven't been able to face them and there are so many. I've been a burden on you and Doreen this last year and it's time I begin paying my way again. I'll start by paying for your accounting. You said it was a slow time of year."

Peter started to awaken to the amount of work that lay ahead as his mother slid seven cardboard boxes of varying sizes away from the rest in the room. All neatly filled with white folders that stood on end so that Peter could look down to see the reams of paper bulging in each one. Each box made uncomfortable lifting and held so much about his parents when he felt like he knew so little. "It looks like things are speeding up." And Claudia smiled for the first time that day.

"You'll do it?"

"Yes. It'll be a treasure hunt. I'll see how wealthy you really are."

"Don't set your hopes too high. Isaac wasn't that good at hiding. It isn't a fortune, just enough for me to start helping myself."

Peter started walking the first box to the trunk of his Mercedes. "No mother, it will be a treasure hunt. I won't know whether to bill you by the hour or by the pound. Either way I stand to make a tidy sum."

"What, no maternal discount?"

"We'll talk price later. A lot of these could just be old bank statements and bills I don't need to see. I've worked for pack rats before. They're always shocked when I make sense of their finances in record time. I don't tell them it is because most of it goes in the trash."

"Well now you've told me so none of it goes in the trash." Peter sensed his mother's uneasiness as she walked behind him as he carried each of the boxes out. She never lifted one herself, but stared at each until it disappeared under the lid of the trunk that she shut without latching each time. "If you don't need some of the papers that's fine, but I would like all of your father's things intact."

"Not to worry mother. I'll find all the things Dad was hiding and put them in order," said Peter as he eased himself into the driver's seat of his Mercedes. He swung his legs in and the engine coughed quickly into a steady purr. "I'll be over later in the week after I've had a chance to look into things."

Claudia closed the door for him and mouthed thank you through the window. Peter threw up his hand in a salute like wave and pulled away from the curb. She stood in the street with her hands on her hips and watched the car roll to a stop before it darted quickly south onto Harlem.

Brett Ramseyer

8

The ringing began before Peter walked in the side door from the garage. He took three quick steps to the kitchen wall phone and lifted the handset from the cradle before his keys finished sliding across the dark granite countertop.

"Sonderlings."

"Peter?"

"*Yes?*"

"It's a mess up here."

"Who is this?"

"Oh, for pity's sake. I'm sorry Peter. It's Rita."

"Rita?" Peter felt himself flush in guilt because he should have known, but could not place the voice.

"Rita VanDuinen. In Pentwater. At your cottage."

"Oh God, I'm sorry Rita, my mind was set on Chicago mode."

"I've been trying to reach you all morning. This is the fifth time I've called since eleven."

"It's only eleven thirty. What's wrong?"

"I know you think I'm prone to overreact, but Bill and I came home this morning from seeing our grandkids overnight. We normally would have only stayed for dinner, but we didn't want to drive home in the weather. There are trees down everywhere our side of Longbridge. We had to weave our way through a lot of timber in the road."

"Is Bill okay?"

"It's not us, Peter. It's your cottage. The white pine has made a terrible mess."

"Are there some limbs down?"

"No, I wouldn't say that." Rita walked over to the window with her hand on her hip and looked over at the Sonderling's sunroom. "The trunk splintered ten feet up and brought the entire tree down into your front room."

"Oh. What kinda damage are we talking about?"

"Bill's over there right now looking over things. He said something about fixing a tarp over a corner of the living room. They're talking two more days of rain right now and he thought he would stop up as much as he could before the next front blows in off the lake."

"It's bad then? I'll have to come up."

"Here Bill's walking in right now. I'll pass you over to him. He's been over there for half an hour. I've just been looking across the lawn. Bill. It's Peter. He wants to know."

Rita slid the phone from her ear and set it in the cold wet hands of her husband. His blunt bass shattered any meager hopes of an inexpensive repair. "She's shot to hell Peter."

"Good morning Bill."

"If you were standing where I am you'd crumple up that 'Good' and throw it away. Your four seasons room let in half of spring last night. The other half will be arriving tonight. Rain's coming for a couple days."

"Rita already gave me the forecast. Is there anything you can do? I can pay you."

"There isn't much I can do Peter. I stapled some canvas around a corner of the living room, but all that glass from your porch is shattered. That room's all outside now."

"What about the tree?"

"Well, I'll tell ya. Remember last summer when Michael bet me he and I could reach around the trunk and join hands and he ended up buying me an ice cream in town?"

"Yeah."

"I should have gotten a ladder and bet him a cone for every rung because it doesn't get skinny very fast and a full thirty feet of that is lying on top of some crystal confetti that was your sun porch. It fell on an angle and the top clipped the eaves and soffit on the northeast corner of the house. Water was running right down the shingles and into the crack. I've patched that up short term, but you will need to do some renovating there."

"Thanks Bill. It sounds like I owe you something anyway."

"Save your money Peter. You'll need it for the restoration."

"I think I'm going to have to drive up."

"That's probably best. You're going to want to see where you're at. Two words of advice?"

"What's that Bill?"

"Chain saw."

***

Isaac released the trigger on the old Craftsman. The bearings were not yet completely worn out, but the circular blade grated shrilly to a stop, metal on metal before the spray of pine dust could settle.

"Son, I've had this old saw for ten years and it still cuts as true as the day I bought it. Always pay for quality, Peter, it's cheaper in the long run."

Peter rolled his eyes, but his turned back hunched over a sawhorse where he hammered a section of framing together that he soon to raised. *Don't worry, Dad, I'm aware of your expertise on cheap* played about the half smile he hid behind his shoulder that he brought up to wipe his forehead. The glaring June sun streaked through the trees and bounced off the light waves of Pentwater Lake on Peter's newly acquired cottage.

"That's why I think you should splurge for the sun porch on this place while we are adding on to it."

"Dad, I don't remember you splurging much when I was a kid."

"What? I made you a new room."

"It was the basement, Dad."

"Right, I built you a new room in the basement."

"All you did was throw up two short racks of studs with a door. I had foundation for two walls left over drywall on one and three different colors of paneling on the other. I've seen more uniform fences made out of old car hoods at the junk yard."

"Eclecticism. I was ahead of my time on design."

"Now you're ahead of me with ideas to spend my money."

"But I am here sweating with you in the sun without a paycheck."

Peter gripped harder on his red handled hammer and pounded on into the afternoon without another thought to money. Contentment filled his days working alongside his closest relative knowing they shared one mind. Each barely spoke more than a grunt while lifting a wall or to call for a nail as the dream of an expanded lake house grew in a latticework of sticks crossing each other, propping, and clinging to each other in the hope of being something greater than themselves.

In the sweltering summer weeks of 1975 Isaac and Peter transformed the humble cottage into a vacation showplace. The living room with fieldstone fireplace reached farther toward the lake and greeted the lawn through the open screened windows of the sun porch. Father and son had worked side-by-side for a month and a half: planning, roughing in, redoing and finishing.

Their mornings started early, but Peter never beat his father to the kitchen. Usually the jolting scent of bacon fat lifted Peter's eyelids. He would sway out to the yard to see Isaac sitting in a white Adirondack chair sipping tea underneath a dockside willow that wept its yellow lashes below the surface of the indolent lake. The yolk of the sun would ooze through the tree thick shore and lay golden shafts across the eaves of the nearly finished cottage and Isaac stared back wistfully. Today would be a final time to run a snapping tape across boards and for brow sweat to trap sawdust like fly paper. These men enjoyed the clean filth of construction that washed off too easily in their evening cannonballs from the end of the dock.

This dream of a house nestled blessed in light and Isaac spoke of it first as Peter crouched low to sit next to him.

Brett Ramseyer

"I never thought a son of mine would have such a home. We've done nice work Peter."

"Thanks Dad. I couldn't have done this without you. You know I owe you more than I could pay."

"Forget it. You couldn't afford my labor anyway. I've enjoyed your company. We haven't seen each other this much since before you started at the University. It's a pity Michael wasn't old enough to help us."

"Doreen couldn't stand the thought of him investigating the use of some power tool while our backs were turned."

"It's probably better we wouldn't want him to cut off his finger with a saw or castrate himself with a drill."

"I should say not!"

"Well Peter you know, these things happen. Doreen is right to keep her boy safe – We'll finish today?"

"Only a few pieces of trim to hang and then clean-up, We'll be able to get you outta here by lunch."

"I'm in no hurry. I'm going to miss this."

"Mom will be glad to see you though."

"Ahh, Dornröschen." said Isaac with twinkling eye.

"Why do you call mom that?"

"She's my sleeping beauty."

"Not the fairytale, Dad. What's the real story?"

"No, not today son, real stories don't end and today is a very happy ending to our summer of building. Let's keep the fairytale and the happiness."

"Alright have it your way, but let's get to work. I promised Doreen I'd bring perch home from Bortell's and have it grilled by the time she and the kids arrived tonight."

The men strode back to the house to don their tool belts only to have Isaac loading his car by ten. Peter lifted Isaac's suitcase into the back before squeezing his father with gratitude.

"Thanks again, Dad." said Peter as he closed the trunk.

***

At ten to midnight Peter reached into the trunk to extract the seventh and last of his mother's cardboard boxes from his Mercedes. He walked it into the cottage and placed it with the rest that already burdened the kitchen table. He sat down and rested his cheek on the cold surface of the table. Thousands of pages lay towering over his ears and the gathering storm front over Lake Michigan rumbled over the nearby dune. He drove maniacally to arrive by four and worked through dinner adding to Bill's patches of green tarp before he felt fairly certain the living room would not flood. Now he sat physically drained, but ready to work some more. He figured even Rita

Come Not To Us

now slept and did not wish to wake her watchful eye with more hammering, sawing or sweeping of glass. He needed a quiet task.

He reached across the table to grab a box and slide it to him. The side that tore in a graceful curve from the top corner to the bottom corner left his lap awash in the receding foam of his father's life. Bills, papers, tax records, letters and history dripped to the floor in a puddle of inconsequence. Peter could not imagine why he could not unroll a black garbage bag from under the sink and start stuffing it full. Instead he started to sort the contents out on the counter.

"A five year old phone bill, precious; three tickets to an opera, folders of ancient yellow newspaper clippings, a birth certificate, a mechanics bill for new brakes, a dinner receipt." Peter itemized aloud to stave off the rising boredom he knew this job would cause. "How much did Mom say she would pay me?"

In minutes a piercing fissure of lightening whitened the lawn and all went dark. A new torrent crashed down from the fast moving storm and the lights around the shore flickered twice before failing.

"Quittin' time," Peter dropped the papers and felt his way through the living room to the threshold of the shattered sun porch. Cataracts curled their way around the tarps to play a tuneless chime on the remaining piles of glass, but it seemed the damaged corner of the house remained water tight. With an overwhelming indifferent languor Peter slumped down on the couch facing the storm to surrender to sleep.

Brett Ramseyer

9

On the top of the yellowing stack of paper clippings stood a white coated man from the past whose eyebrows curved intimately over his piercing black eyes. He stared through the lens and across the decades and over the table covered with raw coffee and stale donuts. His glare caught Peter between groggy sips and pulled him to the headline:

Herr Doktor Peter Kummer entdeckt neues Virus

Historiches Vorschreiten in Stuttgart

Peter who always felt more comfortable over a cipher of figures than letters felt even more lost in the German news clipping. He searched the banner of the page for some numerical bearings when he came across 22 April. 1954.

Peter compelled to understand the knowing gaze slowly placed his half empty mug on the table. He brought his full attention to unfamiliar words that surrounded such an oddly familiar face. Incarnadine helplessness bubbled in his frustration that he, a child of German immigrants, could barely translate cognates like Virus and Doktor to virus and doctor. "Dammit Ma, why wouldn't you ever let Dad speak German. I don't know how I'm supposed to make sense of this mess when you won't let me throw things away and I can't comprehend half of the papers I come across."

He gave up on the top clipping and fanned through the others with his thumb. Most seemed to be small digest items from sidebars with little apparent connection other than the occasional reoccurrence of Kummer, das Hospital, die Klinik, and Gesundheit.

The flash of words landed perplexingly on the only other clipping with a picture at the bottom of the collection. This much newer piece of paper read only *1943* in faded, hand written ink. In the typed caption below the picture it read only *Herr Doktor Sigmund Rascher – Dachau Konzentrationslager.* Doctor Rascher stood behind a steel tub filled with water where a single gaunt face lolling open mouthed lay in the tub. The hollow cheeks of the man looked as if they had not closed around a meal in months and drew a stark contrast to the rubicund jowls of Dr. Rascher who looked down with something that could be confused with concern. His high white forehead wrinkled up above his long straight nose and the tips of his pointed ears seemed to be raised in question.

This doctor, not in white lab coat like the earlier picture, wore the black closely tailored jacket of the SS. The jagged twin lightening bolts of his wicked brethren stood out boldly on his collar. Rascher held the wrist of his bathing patient, but as Peter looked more carefully he noticed Rascher directed his eyes at the chronograph on his own wrist, not the patient. This alien wrist in his hands had no end. It sunk down into the tub in the same bony diameter past the elbow before it disappeared never passing a forearm or bicep. The bathing man appeared in dire straits and the idea of patient submerged below the surface of the water only to sink further into the abyss of victim.

Peter's heart too began to sink at thoughts of cruelty this picture unfolded. He stared again at the SS lapel that seared into him and hovered undiminishing in his closed eyes. He tried to blink it away when he startled from his chair. He stood up straight and pulled the paper inches from his nose. There behind Rascher over his right shoulder in the kink of his neck were those same familiar eyebrows. This time they did not reach through the lens. They, like Rascher, gazed preoccupied with some task that took place behind. The brows faced the opposite direction of the SS doctor, but remained open to the camera. It felt much less of a staged photo than the earlier shot of Dr. Kummer and more like a historical documentation of the events of Dachau. This action shot Peter did not feel prepared to see. He felt his skin cool and his hair stand on end. He flipped quickly back and forth from the clipping of Kummer to Rascher, Kummer – Rascher and to Kummer again. The unmistakable brow left Peter knowing that he was somehow mistaken. He did not know enough. He could not comprehend what flashed right in front of him.

The Rascher clipping had no headline and the copy trailed off in the ragged edge of pulp. Peter could not translate why his Jewish father and mother kept such news moldering away with so many mundane bills and receipts. These seemingly simple boxes filled to capacity with the bureaucracy of their lives had spilled more insight into their past than Peter had heard in his entire life. They stirred infinitely more questions than either parent had ever allowed to happen, but offered no answers. All that they kept hidden from him now sat ominously around this broken vacation cottage, incomprehensible. These illegible letters of conspiring lovers set down in code promised to break who broke them.

***

Peter held the seven letters in one hand pulled over a dusty hard case piece of luggage and stood it up on end. He sat on it like he was accustomed to doing while he hitchhiked in college. Whenever life's dull moments or sudden shifts of ill fortune overwhelmed him he knew he could

Come Not To Us

take to the road for a renewal; he found no other way. He would take the first train out of Chicago in any direction to find a country road. He would sit dressed in his best shirt and tie on his suitcase and wait for fate to brake to a stop next to him, but no sedans stopped in his attic.

The enormity of the letters in his hands had taken the wind from him. He pulled from the last page of correspondence and read an aggressively slanted freehand:

June, 1969

My Dearest Doreen,
I have stopped thinking of US now. I have known from the beginning that we could not be more when what little we have been to each other was more contentment than I deserved in a lifetime. Still, I selfishly long for you. When I stopped by yesterday and saw the twinkle in little Michael's eye as he looked up at you, I knew it was over. You are a mother now. I know very little about women and at times I feel I know even less about you, but I am certain that you held the love of your life in your arms and I was across the room.
Now that is where I will be, in the shadowy corners of every room checking every door looking for you to walk back into my world, but I know it is false hope.

Yours forever in eternity

A violent rush of water charged through Peter's guts as he twisted the letters in his sweating palms. He ran his mind up and down the streets of his neighborhood when he crossed the busy intersection of Chicago and Oak Park Avenue without looking. Two cars lit the dusk red with their taillights and their driver's vitriol twittered with the return of spring birds. In half of the long block between Chicago Ave. and Erie Street Peter stood before the Hemingway birth place.

His disgust exhaled through his flared nostril and half raised lip. He stood with the moist ball of letters that melted like a spring snowball in his pink hands. The Lost Generation landmark seemed inviting on the lower level with a wide stairway leading to an ample double door. The wrap-around porch disappeared around a curve to lure suburban gents to sip shady-ades if they could only ignore the stiff tower thrusting its bawdy shaft into the neighborhood. *It's not discrete, but at least it's honest. I'd have only myself to blame if I ignored a warning like that.*

Peter counted the widows around the arc of the turret and tried to imagine any similarities between Michael and himself. He tried to match one with every pane of glass, but at the moment he could not picture Michael's face or stance or build. For every open window there were two with their shades drawn down and his focus shifted up to a metal rod piercing the sky at the top of the tower. He could only imagine himself slowing spiraling down onto that point impaled and rotating like a hog on a spit. And he spit up his own white frothing stomach unto the lawn before he skulked away wiping this mouth on the cuff of his sleeve. Embarrassed he quickened his pace between each of the trunks on the tree lined street hoping for cover and darkness.

***

Outside the Mercedes a cheering sun shrunk the drops of rain still hanging heavy on sleeping buds in the trees. The season sat loaded, ready to explode if only enough heat could radiate up from the Oceana loam to cause the leaves to snap open like parachutes and descend flutteringly into summer.

Still it was warm and Peter made an acute turn to the west down an oozing track of a road pocked with lines of puddles. The water sat in them silently and blue until his tires pass stirred them up with mud. The splashing mixed together into the soft brown of cream in coffee and sloshed back slowly like a jostled cup, but not before spattering the doors and wheel wells in caramel droplets that appeared white against the black of his car.

Slowing to a crawl around an immense pond that grew out around the depression worn by days of deliveries to a pair of newspaper boxes that apparently held the worlds happenings for the desolate asparagus field behind them, Peter steered far to the right running one side of the car almost into a shallow ditch. The wet ground started to devour the right side and he felt the car sliding dangerously. He instinctively stomped the brake and exacerbated the slide until the chassis rubbed down into the sand leaving the right side wheels dangling six inches below the base of the ditch.

"Sonofabitch"

Worried about his black baby he climbed up out of the car to look. He circled around the front of the car and saw the airborne wheels in the shallow ditch. "This shouldn't be too hard to get out of." He sat back down turned the wheel sharply to the left and pressed down on the accelerator. Instead of pulling him back to the roadway the left wheels cut through the mud until he veered directly toward the ditch. He knew he was lost.

Two homes stood within shouting distance, but they could not be more different. To the north a small two story white home with a front porch, a side sun room and a green roof sat serenely. The garage positioned only a few feet behind Peter's Mercedes just out of the shade offered by two massive maples that lined the street. The well kept lawn tripped over a myriad of flower beds, plantings of ornamental bushes and a half acre garden not yet tilled for the season's plantings. Its familiarity reminded of a house from Peter's street back in Oak Park except its bigger lawn and smaller house evinced the owner's incomparable wealth.

Come Not To Us

To the south the aluminum walls of the mobile home no longer shone with any glimmer of newness. The blue and white siding peeked out around the rusted out hulk of a windowless truck. Suckers around the base of a misshapen black cherry scrapped across the once silver roof. A veritable museum of outdated car parts lay in unsorted piles around the yard which consisted of sand pits now flooded and clumps of wild grasses that grew chest high. A two track cut through it all to stop abruptly at a pile of discarded tires waiting to hatch America's next mosquito borne plague.

The white door opened and a woman stepped out onto the metal landing and descended the four steps in a pair of pink flip-flops smacking below her dirt smeared, yellow calloused feet. Her matching pink shorts clung desperately to her thighs and thin white lines ran up her hips to a powder blue tube top. Her still wet hair hung in rat tails down her naked back and her unmade face had almost an element of freshness to it.

She picked her way through the puddles to the mailbox and bent down revealing an ample chest. Peter began to walk toward the trailer. She raised the red flag slipped a clean envelope through the slit in the front of the corroded black box before she startled at the sight of a strange man across the road.

"Oh! You scared the hell out of me. Don't you know not to be staring all creepy at a woman like that."

"I'm terribly sorry miss, but my car," Peter pointed back, "You see, slid off the road."

She stretched her neck to look over Peter's shoulder and saw the gleaming chrome of the Mercedes hood ornament. "What's a rich fella like you doin' out here in the middle of nowhere in particular?" She said with a half smile. Her eyebrows raised inquisitively and brought her shoulders back with them to create a shape that Peter quickly ran his eyes up and down.

"I'm here to visit an acquaintance about some papers I need translated." The truth seemed innocuous enough, but felt strangely warm to be received without judgment.

She shifted her weight from hip to hip and crossed her arms playfully across her belly that began to peek out below her navel. "What are they in Spanish or somethin'?

"No, German."

"Are you goin' to see that Kraut at the end of the road?

"Yes. Do you know him?"

"No, I'm scured a him. He keeps to hisself. I don't know no one around here that likes him. How you know 'im?"

"Ah, I'll just say he saved my life."

"So you're the guy!"

"Which?"

"There's all kinds of stories floatin' around 'bout him. His face - you're the guy he musta pulled from the fire."

"I don't know anything about that. I haven't known him for long."

She smiled crookedly, "You must be some kind of brave, strong man to get to know him now."

She made her way across the road during the conversation and her elbows brushed up against Peter's arms as she swayed back and forth. Discomfort made the soles of Peter's feet itch. "Listen, do you have a car we can use to pull me out of the ditch?"

"I think I –"

"Morning!" came up across the manicured lawn with the droning putter of a small garden tractor. A bald man in his seventies pulled along side the ditch in his yard, dropped his throttle and leaned across the steering wheel. "You need a pull mister?"

"Yes," said Peter as he turned to face him. "I was just asking – " pointing over his shoulder "if she could pull me out." He turned back to an empty road as the blue and pink shrunk back toward her trailer.

"I'll do it. M'names Dell Bird."

"Peter Sonderling."

"Glad to meet ya. I'll head back to my shed for a chain and have you on your way in a jiffy."

Peter rolled a stone under his toe while he waited. He looked once more at the trailer before kicking the stone across the road skittering into a puddle. Dell was back in a hurry and already crawling around under the car to attach the hook of the chain to something substantial.

"Hey, no need to do that I can get it."

"Nonsense," called Dell from the wheel well. He was lying on his back in the soggy dirt. "A nice looking feller like you needn't be getting your good clothes dirty. You look like you got someplace important to go."

"Important to me, but-"

"I sit by the side of the road waiting to be a friend to man. He'p me up would ya?" He stuck out his meaty paw with every crevice filled in with oil and dust. "I'm not afraid of a little work. I might be retired, but I still know how to work."

"I can see that"

"What's that?" asked Dell as he dropped the ring on the other end of the chain over the ball hitch of the tractor.

"I said, I can see –"

"I been retired for ten years and every day I still wake up at 5:30, eat my oats, listen to the mornin' news on the radio and get to work. It's not a rut, it's a groove I tell ya."

"Nice place you have –"

Come Not To Us

"I put 45 years in doing the same thing every mornin'. I guess I've done every kind of labor there is to offer around these parts. I worked at the iron works down in Rothbury for a time. I worked The Project up south of Ludington when that was goin' up. I've plowed snow for the county road commission. Hell, I even spent some time haulin' pickles for a farmer out in Elbridge. You know, that's the only job I ever been fired from."

"I didn't know."

"Well how the hell could ya," laughed Dell that sounded like air slowly escaping a tire. "We just met. Anyway he fired me all right. I was fit to be tied. I ran the forklift right through his barn loaded down with a full crate of pickles. He cussed me up one side and down the other. I told him it was his own damn fault for not tellin' me the brakes didn't work on the forklift. I was nineteen and full of piss and vinegar. I called him a cheap sonuvabitch for not keepin' up his equipment."

"I can understand why he fired you."

"No that weren't it. He hated me. I was datin' his daughter."

"Did he make you pay for the damage to the barn?"

"In a manner of speaking."

"How's that?

"I married her and been handin' her my paycheck ever since." More air escaped and Dell swung his spry leg over the tractor seat. "Now this is gonna be a team effort here. I haven't exactly won any tractor pulls with this little beast. You'll need to be behind the wheel and give her the gas as I start to pull."

"Let it rip, Dell!" Peter shouted out his open window and they finished the job in less time than it took Dell to discuss his oats. Peter opened his door and walked over to shake his hand. "I was about to ask the girl to help, but I see I found the right man for the job. Thanks."

"Who? Martin?" asked Dell pointing across the street. "I'm not sure I'd give you a plug nickel for that girl. She can't even bend over to pick up a scrap of that shit she's got lyin' around over there and that isn't the half of it. You should hear the stories in this neighborhood about her."

"I hear there are a lot of stories around this bend in the road. Thanks again. I can see you're a busy man so I'll be on my way."

"Don't mention it. I've got some downed limbs in back the house to pick up."

"Me too, thanks Dell."

Brett Ramseyer

10

The familiar brass knocker sounded sharply on the pink door and Peter waited.

He remembered Otto's painstaking gait and turned around. He looked down a narrow stone lined path into a dense growth of stunted cedar and slanting birches. He could make out a small well in the shaded darkness next to a pool of water that disappeared in foliage.

A slow shuffle preceded the cracking of the door seal. Peter turned quickly and even though he had mentally prepared himself for that face he winced. "You k-nocked on my door. Vhy are you jumping?" Peter stood frozen for a moment never ready for this man. "Na ja, zhe face ist hideous. I have jumped in the mirror ten tausend times zince den. Komm Peter. Zince you continually ignore my zign I vill vake you mit kaffee again."

The two men walked through the tight hall into the booth of a kitchen table. Peter sat while Otto again prepared in the kitchen. Peter placed the two clippings on the table and waited with his hands folded. He began loudly, for it was easier to start the conversation while the scarred face rattled behind a partition.

"I've brought some old newspaper clippings I wondered if you could translate for me."

"Are dey auf Deutsch?"

"What?

"Auf Deutsch – in German?

"Oh, yes, yes. Forgive me. I know so little German. That is why I need your help."

"How do you know it ist German, if you know zo little? It could be Dutch."

"No, SS uniforms and it was in my parents' papers. They're both German."

"Den your Vater has done you a disservice not to speak to you in German. It ist zhe langvage of Siegfried, Nietzsche, Wagner, und Bismarck. Dhere ist much room for pride."

"My mother didn't think so and Dad never disobeyed."

"Schrecklich."

"Whatlich?

"Terrible – Vhat ist zhis you vant translated?" Otto used his cane to push himself down into the tight bench seat across the table from Peter. He picked up the brittle paper and squinted at the pictures. His focus immediately locked onto the bold headline and he read aloud in a guttural

whisper. "Meine Brille, bitte." And he pointed to the half wall behind
Peter's head. He saw a pair of half spectacles with wire ear loops that
curved all the way back forward. He placed them in Otto's hand who did
not bother to look up. He began to run his finger along each line of copy.

"Well what does it say?"

"Qviet, vun cannot conzentrate."

"Sorry, I'll wait."

"Danke."

Peter began slowly thrumming his fingers noiselessly on the
hideously speckled formica of the table top and counting the audible ticks of
a green clock hanging in the tiny den behind him. *124...125...126.*

"It zeems zhis Doktor Kummer discovered a virus new to zhe
1950's. He verked in a hospital in Stuttgart. It vas vun of zhe first
discoveries of its kind in Germany after zhe vor. Dey claim it ist historical."

"So he cured many people?"

"Vielleicht – perhaps. It only reads zhat he discovered a rare
intestinal virus. No verd on zhe outcome. Razer mundane news to keep for
turty years."

"Yes it's probably nothing, his face just struck me. What of this
other?" And Peter pulled the other clipping from beneath that of Dr.
Kummer. Otto looked down and Peter followed the old man's eyes. They
targeted the violent SS on the doctor's lapel and Otto's lips began to pull
back and he placed the paper on the table and looked up at Peter his eyes
alight.

"Ja stimmt, I know of zhis Doktor Sigmund Rascher."

"What do you know?"

"More dan you can bear zu hear."

"I've spent 39 years of not hearing anything. It is time that I bear
something from the past. Read it to me."

"I needn't read it zu know zhe shtory. He ist infamous, like Josef
Mengele only not mit Zwillinge. He verked mit kalt. Zhat is klar in zhe
picture."

"Please help me understand, don't confuse me more. Swillinga?"

"Ja, Zwillinge – tvins. Mengele took Jewish tvins at Auschwitz and
experimented on zhem for science. Rascher did much of zhe same at
Dachau."

"What's Dahkow?"

"It ist a town, but vas a concentration camp outside München. It vas
mostly for political prisoners at first, but as zhe zecond vor vore on more
Jews verked zhere. Rascher verked on zhe Jews zo zu speak."

"Worked on - what are you talking about?"

"He vas an SS man, nutting could shtop his qvest for ideas to help
zhe cause. Zhe Russian front vas freezing German soldiers to death faster

60

dan all zhe ill aimed Russian bullets ever could. Ve needed a cure for zhe kalt. Rascher saught he could zupply zhat cure mit vhat he called "Terminal Experiments."

"Terminal -- as in dead?"

"You are undershtanding qvickly. Zhe common propaganda shtarted vell before zhe vor about Jews. Dey vere filsy rats und Rascher und Mengele naturlich, made dem dheir lab rats, mit Himmler's approval."

Peter's ashen face turned toward Otto's eyes. His jaw hung slack and he sat motionless and weak. He could not speak his mouth now dry.

"You look like zhe man in zhe picture. Should I continue? You could barely handle zhe shtory of zhe pistol vhipped Jewess. I don't dink you are ready for zhis.

"Who's ever ready? Go on." cracked off Peter's desiccated tongue while he sat wide-eyed and perspiring.

"I do not know all zhe methods, but zhis picture shows vun. Zhe Doktors vould place zhe subjects into a tub of ice vater und drop zhe body temperature. Zhey qvickly found zhat an average human whose core temperature dropped below five und twenty degrees centigrade vould lose consciousness und die. Vhen vinter came zome vere shtrapped to gurneys und placed outside naked for tventy or more hours."

"They would just freeze them and let them die?" said Peter picturing his father lying naked in the snow.

"Of course not - zhe point vas to revive zhem to save German soldiers. Vunce zhe subjects vere prepared mit kalt zhe experiments began. Many vays of varming zhe subjects vere done. Many vere unnecessarily cruel, but I dink zhose vere done to cut zhe boredom of zhe day, like a child cooking ants mit a magnifying glass. I do not dink zhat zome of zhem vere ever intended to be tried on good German soldiers."

"What did they do?" asked Peter unable to stop the torrent he unleashed.

"Again I do not know all zhe details, but vun completely unsuccessful method vas dual irrigation. Near shteaming vater vas forcibly injected srough zhe rectum und mouth to fill zhe gastric cavity from both ends. Zhey believed varming zhe body from zhe inside out vould verk more qvickly, but all zhat vas ever done vas to cook zheir organs and kill zhem mit shock."

Peter looked down at the steam rising from his coffee. He put it down on the table and pulled his hands away. His stomach snap rolled over his esophagus. "It was just terminal torture!"

"It vasn't alvays zo cruel. Zhe most successful method of reviving vas a varm bath vhere zhe temperature vas slowly increased to reduce shock." Otto's fingers flicked back and forth over the edge of the clipping playfully and he looked blankly over Peter's shoulder as if he flipped through the old picture album of his memory recounting glory days.

"Rascher alzo verked mit experiments on zhe effects of atmospheric pressure und many doctors verked on genetics, eugenics und sterilization. Zhe perfect human being vas being engineered and he vould have pure Aryan blood, but not Rascher."

"How could there be anything pure about that man? He sounds like all the evil of the Nazi party wrapped in a white coat of pseudo-science."

"Zome felt him a hero, but zhe Gestapo found zhat he and his vife Karoline vere frauds. She vas sterile and to prove zhey shtill met zhe shtrict shtandards of SS purity zhey zimulated a pregnancy for her and zecretly adopted a child. It vas a scandal of undoing und he vas later shot as a prisoner at Dachau."

"Shooting is too good for devils like that."

"It ist too good for us all in zhe end. Ve all have our wrongs."

"What are yours?"

"It ist a list zu lang zu nummer."

"Are yours from the wars?"

"Nein, zhose years vere chaos, but I regret nutting from zhem. I regret not seeing zhe faces of my children."

"I didn't picture you a father."

"Ich auch – zhat ist vhat I told Anna, my zecond vife."

"You had to fight with her to keep the maternal instincts at bay."

Otto chuckled and gave his coffee a slow stir. "Are you familiar mit Lady Macbeth?"

"Shakespeare?" Otto gently nodded. "I did the obligatory reading in high school, but nothing more. I think she wanted her husband to kill somebody and then she regretted it or something."

"You need to be a more careful reader. Her husband had his own ambitions as I did und his vife gave zhe final push for him zu do it. Zhere ist a line vhere she boasts how she vould tear her childs toothless gums from her own nipple and dash out its brains if she had svorn zu do zo."

"A real princess."

"She vanted to be qveen actually. Vell, Anna vas more determined dann Lady Macbeth und I did not need convincing. Zhe difference vas more about zcraping dann dashing."

"What do you mean?"

"Abortions – two of zhem here in zhis kitchen."

Peter's face curled up around his nose and he rubbed his tear ducts in disbelief. "How could you?"

"Zhe light vas better in here. It ist a zimple, but delicate procedure."

"Not the kitchen, how could you play God like that, like Rascher. You're no better than him – a murderer."

Come Not To Us

"It does not take vun long to discover during vor zhat zhere ist no Gott. His tvilight hast come. Ve mortals are left to enact our vill on zhis earth as ve see fit. I zaw fit not zu allow my race zu continue und es ist zo. I am zhe only Gott I know."

"You're a God damn lunatic! Disgusting."

"Do not vorry, he cannot punish you for taking His name in vain. He ist as impotent as I in my old age." Otto dabbed his right eye with a red paisley handkerchief and loudly emptied his nose into it before crumpling the cloth into the pocket of his faded overalls.

"You really think this is funny don't you?"

"Vhat can I zay. I love zhe company of misery. It heats my heart zu zee you tvist your face zo painfully at my beliefs. Only zhe Germans have zhe verd for dis – Schadenfreude – und I do zo joy in your pain. Vhy do you dink I zo readily invite you in, make you Kaffee zu trinken, und entertain your qvestions? Komm? Vhy?"

"Because you're the sickest bastard I've ever seen."

"Und forget it not because zhe zight of you scratches at my palms. Zhe smell of your inferior Jewish Arschloch singes my nose." Otto's anger rose up from the table like a tsunami. Peter unknowingly started the silent earthquake deep in Otto's ocean of hatred. Otto's pretended hospitality had coaxed him into a receding sea and now stood poised to pound him into the sand and Peter did the only thing he could.

Peter reached across the table grabbed the white frothing wisps of hair and rammed the old man's face into the table. Blood exploded out of Otto's nose and Peter threw the reddened face backward into his seat. "Smell that you ancient Nazi shit. It's the scent of Jewish militancy. We're not afraid any more and your breed is dying out."

"My breed ist dying because I cut it from its mutter's vomb. My foggy ancestory vas zu big of a risk und I vas not villing to bring more Jewish blood into zhe verld."

"You're a Jew!" burst out incredulously from Peter.

"I am a German. My grandmutter vas a whore und I did vell to root out zhe fruit of her vandering. How does zhat sit mit your Gott?"

"You –"

"Zhe answer is indifference, not caring, abandonment. Zhere have been entire decades vhere I have sat und vaited for a reprisal und nutting. Ja, your Gott does not even have zhe shtrength zu kill me. No more zhan you have zhe power zu scare me. I vill not die of a bloody nose. I have faced no misfortune I did not do myself und I have celebrated no victory for vhich I needed zu pray."

"You're a vile excuse for an organism."

"Are you disgusted because you dink I am mitout faith?"

"No, I shrink from you because you are bereft of even one cell of humanity. You take joy in my pain, in the pain of others and do so with brazen disregard for all that is decent."

"Do not dink for even vun moment zhat my greatest joy is anyding less dann my own pain. How else could I have risen every morning to vash my face mit kalt vater und lift my chin up to zhe mirror to zee dis lump of flesh hanging from my jaw. Und make no mistake, Gott did not punish me mit zhis. Zhis I have done myself und ja, I laugh at your infinitesimally small pain. It ist a joke. You veep und shtumble srough zhe dark mit a pistol because your vife has shtrayed. Vhen you hold your own vife in your arms und kiss her flaming face hoping zhat your own tears vill put out zhe fire zhat hast consumed her corpse, you may shpeak zu mir of pain. Vhen your own cheeks have dripped down your chin to shplatter sizzling on zhe concrete mit less ache dann zhe shriek of 'Evaline' across your lips, you may shpeak zu mir of suffering."

***

"Why did you kiss Dad on the mouth at his funeral?"

A long pause crackled over the receiver while Peter waited. He stared at the boxes in the cottage kitchen awaiting a flood from the past to flow across Lake Michigan through the channel and up into the battered porch. The phone's handset felt heavy and he reached up to hold it to his ear with both hands.

"That's not something I'm ready to talk about Peter."

"Dad's been dead for over a year."

"Don't say 'dead'."

"It doesn't matter how I say it, so long as I say something, anything about the truth. I've got boxes here filled with things you've never had the courage to say and I don't even know what I'm looking at."

"You're wrong. It matters how you say things."

"But you never say anything about the past. Since Dad died I feel I know less and less about him because you had him so scared in his lifetime of telling me anything from the past. Now you're teasing me with the possibility of learning something about you and Dad with all these boxes. There are documents and articles in German and I can't speak a word. Why didn't you and Dad ever speak to me in German and teach me of my history."

"Because I didn't want it to be your history. It is an ugly language spoken in an ugly time. And believe me I learned in Germany *how* you say things is extremely important."

"What does that mean? You've said things like that my entire life. I've always known they were the tip of some story on your tongue that you just cut off. It's always made me feel like conversations with you were over the phone. You have always been hundreds of miles away from me speaking in clipped phrases, saying as little as possible. For once tell me a story, the whole story and the devil take the consequences. I'm practically forty years old. I can handle it." breathed Peter into the phone like a deflated balloon.

"I know how old you are."

"Just tell one damn story, *how* saying things matters."

"I don't know if –"

"For me."

"I can."

"For Dad." Peter waited. He heard Claudia pull a sniffle through her nose and swallow it down like a pill.

"I learned it from Bettina…"

Peter feeling her hesitance and the distance growing between grabbed onto the only rope he had to pull her back to the story. "Who's Bettina?"

"We called her Blutig Bettina. She was the only Aufseherin in the camp.

"Aufseherin?"

"Female guard – we called her bloody because once she was angered she wouldn't stop even if you were bleeding."

"What did she teach you?"

"She taught me to be careful of how I speak and when. She was a fat prostitute from Munich. She used to joke that she would work the streets outside the Frauenkirche because she said that all the men got stiff at the thought of a women's church and were more ready to hire someone to take it out on. She'd laugh and spit through the gaps left from her missing eye teeth and smack her flashlight against her left palm. She'd always walk in circles too, like a buzzard around her prey. When the male guards would see her circling some poor girl they would start to gather around and place bets on how many times she would strike the girl before she bled and there were still other wagers on how many blows after."

"One girl, Jutta Neider, said she knew a trick that could save my life if old Blutig Bettina started circling me. She said I should watch carefully when she was about to strike and immediately bite open my lip to run blood. She said it had worked for her one day behind the barracks. Jutta said that she took one blow to the jaw from Blutig's flashlight, bit down hard rolled on her back and pretended to be unconscious. Jutta said Bettina only swung twice more in the stomach and went back to roving patrol, but I knew it wasn't true. Bettina loved blood and the more she unleashed from a girl the more frenzied her attack became."

"I overheard a guard ask her one night as she skulked through the shadows between the rows of barracks why she didn't ever turn on her flashlight to see where she was going. She unscrewed the cap of her black beauty and poured a dozen of small bearings into her hand. 'Birdshot' she told him, 'packs a bigger knock than batteries.'"

"The guard looked at her and said, 'Bettina, du bist eine böse Hexe.'"

"Bettina just laughed and said, 'Witch am I? Is that why you're always paying me to ride your broomstick?'"

Peter interrupted confused, "But why wouldn't the girl tell you the truth about a woman like that?"

"Jealousy. The camps were a place where everyone's true self came out. There was no place to hide human frailty. Bettina felt her power there when she was accustomed to having none. Jutta who was once a beautiful girl saw her social standing fall like a meteor under Nazi rule and even in the camps she could not gain favor with the guards as she thought I had done. Her head was asymmetrical that appeared lopsided without hair. Mine was more round so I did not sweat in roll call square under heavy loads like Jutta. I worked in the hospital and she hated me for it."

"I told Jutta I knew she was just jealous that I had a less physically taxing job and she was trying to trick me into falling under the blows of Blutig Bettina. I no more than said her name and I felt her circling us. Bettina had overheard my comments and began to spiral closer to us. Jutta backed away quickly looking down before she melted behind the gathering flock of guards."

"Blutig Bettina!" said the corpulent whore. "Blutig Bettina? Blutig Bettina. How does that sound you rat stink Jew?" She was not angered by the name because she reveled in hearing it whispered in the women's barracks while she walked at night. It was in her mind an awe inspiring name to instill fear and respect. If she commanded an extensive vocabulary she might have added the Venerable Blutig Bettina.

"It – it sounds-" quivered Claudia.

"It sounds like you're scared you Scheiße." Bettina smiled as she paced in her dizzying circle behind Claudia. "Are you scared? Are you, Hure!"

"Ja." whispered Claudia.

"Ich kann nicht hören."

"Ja, Frau Bettina."

"Nein, nicht 'Frau Bettina.' Sagst du, 'Böse, Blutig Bettina.'"

"Ja. Böse Blutig Bettina."

"Lauter, Hure!" Screamed Bettina.

"Ja, Böse Blutig Bettina," said Claudia feeling her neck burn where hair would have stood on end.

"Sehr gut. You have learned an important lesson. You have passed your first examination on *how* to say my name properly. It is time to see if you can pass the second course. You see Jew, once a month I really am Blutig Bettina. We'll see if you have a taste for it."

Claudia buckled to the floor as a sharp flashlight blow hit behind her knee. A stark white thigh pocked with fat flashed in front of her and the circle of aroused guards closed in to watch.

Brett Ramseyer

Come Not To Us

11

Perfect lake afternoons astound with their exact sameness to all the other perfect lake afternoons in history. They shine backward in the boyhood photos of a vacationing Hemingway near a dock where calming ripples stand frozen in time. They stretch back to paintings famous and unknown with the same slothful clouds that hang for an eternity in a crisp sky without moving even though the breeze coming in off the water is cool and quick. The tree tops sway back and forth like impatient children at a church picnic waiting for the pastor to finish the blessing so they can spring across the lawn to swallow whole breasts and thighs of barbecued chicken between golden ears of butter dripping corn.

Such mind numbing similarity makes all who sit and look at such days raving ninnies. They sit in their chairs looking, listening, breathing before suddenly they snap up to wander under a shade row of maples and seek out some other wide-eyed moron feeling the same amazement.

"This is the best goddamn day I've ever seen," comes blathering out of nodding heads backed only by a slew of platitudes like "Gorgeous!", "Beautiful!" and "Unbelievable!" Their tight smiles need only merit incredulity that their heads do not snap off at the jaw and tumble down to the water's edge to rock aimlessly back and forth like beach balls in the eddies.

The beach ball rolled over to watch Peter in the form of Rita in a cheerful floral print dress. She just must see the damage, but she would only admit to others that she stopped by to check the progress.

"Well God's day to you Peter," simpered out of Rita with such enthusiasm that Peter couldn't help but smile even with the heavy load of limbs he pinned beneath his own. "Isn't this just the finest day we've ever been blessed with? I was a mite surprised not to see you out here yesterday heaving those big limbs off a that porch, because Lord knows well begun is half done. I heard the saw so I just had to make my way over to see how much progress you've made. I mentioned something to Bill about coming over to see if you were all right yesterday, but he said, 'Sometimes a man needs to set and let that kind of work soak in before he starts.' I can understand that because you sure have a powerful lot of work before you can even think of rebuilding. Are you rebuilding? I hope so. I always envied the look of that sun porch on sunny November days when all the leaves are down and there's nothing to block His glorious light from shining down. I've wanted one for myself on those days because the wind off the water would chap your face before you had a chance to pucker. I asked Bill to build me one of those porches and he said… You know, come to think of it he said the same thing. He said, 'Sometimes a man needs to set and let that kind of work soak in before he starts.' She laughed from her belly in a clear bell-like way before snorting to a stop through her nose.

Removing his blue leather gloves Peter shrugged the short sleeve across the sweat collecting around his mouth. He stood straight on his left foot while his right leg bent. This set his hips askew where he planted his fists holding the gloves' loose fingers behind him like the tail feathers of a drooping rooster.

"Where is old Wild Bill?"

"Fishing. He churned out the channel on *Calvary* around 4:30 this morning. He and his buddies said they'd be out fourteen miles and be back by supper with more than they could eat in a week. Since you'll be around awhile I'll save you a pike or two out of the smoker."

"Thanks Rita. That's the life, isn't it? I pity the poor saps who have to grunt like this all day."

"Oh I don't know my Father used to say, 'He who sweats all day always earns his pay.'"

"My Dad had a saying too."

***

"Your work will set you free, Peter."

"But Dad, Wendell always gets there early to hurry up the guys to pick teams. If I'm late they always stick me on the loser's team."

"So join them and make them winners."

"How can I? My fingers are always so cramped I can barely grip the bat. Everybody groans when I join the team."

"I know. Wendell is a dummkopf, but his shortcoming will not get in the way of you learning your math homework."

"But school's almost out for the summer. May I please go now?"

"Nonsense, none of those boys will play for the Cubs and you, you will be a math genius. No one will pick you last in arithmetic."

"No girls pick you first because of arithmetic, but they will if I hit a home run," and Peter made a phantom stroke that would have made Ernie Banks proud.

"Girls? What need have you for girls? You're only eleven."

"I'm ten," corrected Peter.

"What?" an alarmed look came across Claudia's face as she wiped dishes at the sink.

Isaac held up his hand at her and winked at Peter. "You see I skipped my math lessons to meet my cousins in the park. A good father doesn't allow his son to make the same mistakes. Your work will set you free."

Come Not To Us

Peter traded his glove for a pencil and set back to work. Claudia kept her eyes quietly focused on Isaac while she mechanically placed the last plates in the cupboard. Isaac placed his hand between Peter's shoulder blades and looked on approvingly for a time.

"Very good fifty-three divided by seven is seven point five. Seven point five what?"

"The teacher says we only need to go to the tenths place."

"Is that good enough for you?"

"Yes."

"Then it should be good enough for me. You're free."

Peter glugged down his last two inches of milk and careened toward the door. He snatched his blue cap from the peg and started to run.

"Peter!" shouted Claudia. He stopped with a sheepish turn.

Isaac walked between them and said, "Be sure to beat Wendell."

"I will," smiled Peter.

"And Peter," said Isaac sternly.

"Yes, Dad."

"I love you."

"You know how much I love you, Dad?"

"How much?"

"Seven point five seven," and Peter ducked out the door.

"Ha-ha no tenths place for my boy. Hundredths. Thousandths. Ten-hundred-thousandths if he likes. I swear Claudia we've raised a genius," gloated Isaac as he grabbed his wife by the waist and locked his fingers together behind her. He began to swing her around when she planted her hands on his chest and pushed herself free.

"I can't believe you!" leveled Claudia.

"What?"

"You can't play the fool with me. He's getting older now. There is no longer room for loose facts."

"What eleven?" I fixed zhat."

"Fixed *what?*"

"The arithmetic. It was all a lesson in hard verk."

"Hard *vhat?!*"

"Verk?"

"Not verk, dammit, w-w-w-work!"

"My accent? I didn't slip with him and who cares? He knows we're German. Are we hiding *that* now?"

"Yes, as much as we can *that*. I scrub until I break my nails to wash the filth that Germany heaped on me."

"You're not alone in your suffering, but the Nazis chained me, not Germany."

"Germany was all too glad to stand by and let it happen. I curse them all."

"And your husband?"

"Who teaches his son the murderer's mottos, yes."

"Claudia you've lost it. What motto?"

She closed her eyes and shivered at the picture in her memory. The black iron in front of a low oppressive sky of white stood as stark in her lids as a construction paper cut-out on a frosty window. She opened her eyes again and whispered, "From the gate, Isaac, Arbeit macht frei." She fell into a ball in his arms sobbing. "Work makes you free, that terrible joke. I can still hear that hideous and cruel laughter that those – those specters that would have scared the devil to cold ashes blew at me. But no – you teach it to your Jewish son like it is some great wisdom passed down through the ages to be carried on forever. Such iniquity should not be in you Isaac. Peter will not carry on their wickedness."

Somber and regretful, Isaac backed away from his wife, turned and sat on the table. "I saw the sign too and there was a long time I prayed hourly for their dead freedom, but I didn't die." Isaac stood up. I didn't see the gate until I had already been penned inside. I read it backwards.

ᴀʀʙƎⁱᴛ

ⁱƎʁᖵ ᴛHↃᴀM

I used to tell myself that it was written in Russian because Germany would never betray me like that. Sometimes, I still wonder if I believe such a land could do those things to me."

Isaac looked down at his hands and then back to Claudia. "I've held the very bars of that gate in my hands. I felt their cold indifference to me and I've awakened at night rattling them while the guards filled my back with machine gun fire. I must take the good from that evil place and make my life of it or I'll forever be imprisoned there."

A pregnant pause hung between them before Claudia could answer. "No good can come of evil, Isaac, and I'll not have you filling our son with any of their *facts*. Next you'll be telling him that the distance between his eyes or the shape of his nose make him better, worse, dumber, smarter, worth living more than the neighbors."

"He's your son Claudia and I'll not interfere, but you're wrong," and Isaac turned to walk to the bedroom. "That's not the story I want to tell."

***

Come Not To Us

"Daddy tell me a story out of your own mind," whispered little Pe with his covers pulled up tight to his chin and his eight plump fingers sticking out like a wiggling bowtie.

"It's been such a long day at work I don't know if I have any stories in my mind today," said Isaac as he stood one pillow on end against the headboard. He sat and swung one leg atop the covers.

"Yes you do. Tell me the one about the dwarf and the princess."

"It's so scary. Do you think you can sleep after such a story?"

"It's not scary. It's make believe."

"It's scary to me and as real as the nose on your face. I don't know that I should be telling such a story. Your mother doesn't like such tales."

"She's not here. Please Dad."

"All right, all right, where should I start?"

"You know where to start, the village. You always start in the village."

"Ah yes, the village. It was not your typical village and it was filled not with your typical people. It was an extraordinary village where thirty-two houses standing row on row were split down the center by a lonely gravel street, but it was a street that did not lead anywhere. It went forward and it went backward, but there was no place to travel, for around the village were the high castle walls and the moat filled with terrible man-eating water that lay black like oil. It bubbled in the heat of the day and at night was rumored to have slithered into some of the houses like a snake to pull some of the villagers from their beds to prepare them for its breakfast."

Peter's eyes opened wide and he bounced under his covers. "Now the villagers, tell me about the villagers."

"The villagers were a peculiar lot of characters to be sure. Each was unique in their walk of life, but here they were all made dwarfs, dwarfs who walked dead on their feet waiting for the day they could vault the castle walls to travel to their own homes all across the land. It was with these dwarfs that a special dwarf, named Micha, lived and worked through days that felt like centuries."

"Why couldn't he leave, Daddy?"

"You always ask that. Just listen. None of the new made dwarfs could leave because they had all been captured by an evil king and his henchmen. They roved the countryside in shining black boots to tear the people from their beds and throw them into his crowded village. Then they would be free to steal all their riches at their leisure to add to their piles of gold."

"At the village the king made the dwarfs work day and night baking more bricks for his walls, but the jobs most feared were for his most merciless sorcerer named Sigmund. Sigmund cast spells and incantations that tried to make men breathe without air and live without heat. He was dressed from head to toe in a black satin cape that hung loosely about his body. A sinister hood hung low over his eyes that were not eyes like you and me, but were two fiery bits of lightening bolts that the devil himself had stolen from God's sky and had crammed deep into Sigmund's head. It was from this sorcerer that Micha knew he must escape before those eyes reached out with their powerful charge and zapped the life from his body, but it would not be so easy."

"Sorcerer Sigmund had a keen eye for devious dwarfs who looked like they had discovered a way over the king's wall and he was quick to snatch them and begin his spells. It was this kind of dwarf he saw in young Micha and one winter when the wind from the north froze birds right to the clouds he cast a wicked spell that pinned Micha to a tree. Micha struggled and fought, gritted his teeth and screamed, but he could not break the invisible bonds that left him in the cold."

"That night the most furious snowstorm that ever grew from the North Sea swept down on Micha and in minutes snow covered his toes. He struggled and pulled with all his might, but Sigmund's spell was too strong. The white crystals swirled and fell and were soon up to his waist. In an hour Micha screamed with all the energy he had left and tugged mightily at the tree, but the snow piled in on top of him stealing all light. It was black and Micha's head dropped into a frigid and exhausted sleep."

"How'd he wake up Daddy," said Peter unable to wait.

"He awoke slowly, first at his feet, up his legs, over his chest and then to his eyes. Micha saw her."

"The Princess, Daddy?"

"Yes, Peter the Princess. She hovered over Micha like the warmest sunshine he had ever known. Her arms wrapped around him and he could feel his blood rise back into his limbs. His strength came back to him while she held him in warmth. He tried to speak to her to ask her name, but his dry throat cracked and fell silent. Her eyes looked down on him peculiarly and her lips pressed down on his in a beautiful kiss. Micha closed his eyes while his body filled with the energy of ten thousand stars. He smiled. When his eyelids popped open she had vanished without a trace, but the tree and the castle walls were nowhere around. He looked down at himself and no longer had the body of a dwarf. He rose quickly looked into the distance and began to run in his search of the Princess."

12

The phone nagged Peter from across the room. He sounded his disgust like a clearing of phlegm from his throat. He tossed down his papers and pencil with a slap and pulled the turtle brown handset off the wall. Doreen's "Hello." Curled up the right corner of his lip and sent deep furrows above his eyebrow while his fingers played violently with the circles of the cord by crushing them flat between his fingers.

"Hi," he said curtly.

"I called to check up on you. It's been a few days. The kids wanted me to call and make sure you weren't lying under a tree."

"I'm fine."

"Is the damage extensive? Rita called me and made it sound pretty bad. She said you looked tired."

"You know Rita. She talks a lot."

"The damage?"

"The sun porch is gone."

"Oh Peter, you and your Dad built that together."

"I know."

"Can it be saved?"

"No, it's a complete loss on the porch and the smashed eaves don't look good. First, clean-up will take some time. It took two days just to clean up the pine that brought it all down."

"Which tree was it?"

"Remember the white pine we always rake up the needles from and you suggest we cut it down every spring? Well, I'm still raking needles out of the house and it cut itself down pretty much."

"The whole thing?" asked Doreen in disbelief.

"There is still ten to fifteen feet of trunk sticking up out of the ground with all blonde splinters at the top. I may leave it up as a monument to what once was."

"I'd think you'd just mow it down after how it smashed your porch."

"Yeah, I might do that."

"When do you think you'll be home?"

"I haven't thought about it."

"Well, what have you been doing? I'm at home here with two kids and you've run off with barely a note forwarding address."

"Fine, you're working two jobs there and I'm working two jobs here."

"What eating and sleeping? Come on Peter, you clean-up the tree, you patch the roof and come home. The kids need a father around too."

"But you don't need a husband, is that it?" said Peter his anger rising up in him like a hungry flame. "'Wash my car, feed the kids, mow the lawn, drive Claudie to school, now get the hell away from me.' Is that your recipe for my return? I'm to do your bidding then chain myself up in the basement at night. You selfish –"

"Go ahead Peter, say it."

"I don't need to. You know what you are."

"Bitch, go ahead, bitch. You can say it can't you?"

"That wasn't the word I was thinking, but you're more self aware than I thought. Keep going *honey*, tell us more about yourself."

"Asshole. You're a spineless asshole."

"Yeah, that's right tell me about how a real man would have hit you. How he would have called you names and thrown you down. I've never laid a finger on you and you act like it's my biggest vice."

"At least I could feel something then. Instead I'm married to some – some zombie. Most of the time you're off skulking in some hidden corner avoiding everything and when you are around you're about as noticeable as a pane of glass. People see right through you and you let them ignore you. I swear I walk by you and hardly notice you anymore."

"Maybe if I were a mirror you'd be more apt to look."

"Don't even start with me because I *actually* give a damn about myself. I run a shop and I sell. That means selling flowers, me, and the whole idea of a beautiful life. I don't sit in a basement counting other people's money."

"You know what Doreen? You enjoy your beautiful life. Go to your little shop that my basement counting paid for and sell yourself all day long. You never know. Maybe you could look up an old client –" and Peter's right ear exploded in the clatter of Doreen's anger. She had slammed the phone down and cut the line on him in disgust, but she could not stop him from screaming his finale. "- he could give you the black eye you so desperately desire."

***

"What happened to your eye?" asked Peter as he set down his suitcase next to the bed. His concern was quite confused as he sat down on the bed and brushed the loose strands of Doreen's hair up off her forehead and held her face softly behind the jaw.

"Oh it's nothing," she said through a wet nose and bloodshot eyes. "It's just a clumsy pregnant woman, stumbling around the house."

"What? Stumbling onto your face?"

"Does it look bad?" and she pushed past Peter off the bed and walked into the bathroom. She flipped on the light and stood up on her tiptoes as she leaned in close to the mirror. "Ahh," she squealed as she squinted closer to the mirror. "I look like hell."

Peter pulled the small end of his tie out of the loop before he tugged it under the collar from around his neck. He undid his top button and ran his hand around his chafed neck. He craned backward to look through the crack left in the door. "Are you all right?"

"My eyes are all puffy, to go along with the rest of me," joked Doreen.

"You're six months pregnant. What do expect. You look beautiful. Some women really enjoy their pregnancy you know," said Peter as he came up behind Doreen and wrapped his arms around her waist.

"Stop! You're going to make me fall."

"In love with me all over again."

"You're in a good mood for someone who came home to a battered wife."

"What happened anyway?"

"Oh it was nothing. I had the dirty laundry basket in my hands, slipped on my way down the stairs and hit my eye on the rail."

"You poor baby, come here and let papa kiss it better for you."

"Are you practicing?"

"To be a papa?"

"Yes."

"I guess." Peter leaned down and pressed his lips gently on Doreen's swelling eye. She winced and gave him a disgusted glare.

"Well you still need a lot of work."

"Sorry, that needs ice or you're going to be looking out from underneath a pork chop for an eyelid for the rest of the week."

"Could you get me some," said Doreen from out a pouting lip

"Sure." And Peter was walking down the stairs to the kitchen. He opened the freezer rummaged through some freezer burned meat. Upstairs it sounded like Doreen was scrambling through the closet herself before it stopped in a loud thump. Peter yelled up the stairs, "Careful or you are going to have a matching set of those." He finally found something the right size and smiled, closed the door and walked up the stairs.

"What is that?" exclaimed Doreen.

"Pork chop."

"I'm not putting that on my eye."

"Like I said, pork chop now or pork chop later. What's it going to be?"

"Alright, give it here. Owww! That hurts, he – he- he."

"Give it time to work. What were you storming around through up here?"

"Nothing, what are you talking about?"

"I heard you thumping through the closet or something."

"I think your convention has numbed part of your brain. I didn't make any noise while you were downstairs. How was the tax seminar?

"Taxing."

"Did you learn all the loopholes that will make us millions?"

"They may make my clients millions, but for us it is only a few hundred at this point."

"Well maybe you could accelerate it into the thousands pretty soon. We will be new parents in a few months and we haven't even started on putting together a room for the baby."

"That reminds me," said Peter springing over to his suitcase. "I was early for my flight at JFK and this kept staring at me from the gift shop window. It cost too much, but I was missing you and thinking about my son, so I bought it and left the change." He unzipped his pack and tossed a fluffy blue bear into his wife's lap.

"You're sure it's a boy huh?"

"One-hundred-percent positive."

"What if she doesn't like blue?"

"He will. How's that eye?"

"I'll live."

"How'd you fall down the stairs and not land on the baby?"

"My face broke the fall. Remember?"

"I remember. Let me see it." Doreen lifted the pork chop slowly off her eye. "Oo, it's turning black. How long ago did you do this?"

"Not long before you came home."

"Well I won't be gone for that long any time soon and I'll be around to keep an eye on you."

"Just what I need, you following me around with a pillow all day." Doreen left the pork chop thawing on the plastic bag on the bed and walked into the bathroom. "I'm taking a shower. Don't leave your suitcase next the bed."

"I love you too, sweetie."

"Yah."

Peter groaned and set his suitcase on his side of the closet. He unbuttoned his cuffs and shirt front while he kicked his shoes off unto the rack. He shrugged off the button down before reaching over his head and grabbing his undershirt by the neck and pulling it over his head. He wadded both articles into a ball and tossed them onto the basket filled with dirty laundry.

13

The next morning Peter was never so happy to have a hammer in his hand. The fight with Doreen hung fresh in ears so he swung the tool claw first into the light dry wood. Splinters shot up at his eyes and rained down below his feet. For the first three hours he did not labor with the intent to salvage much of his work. He simply planted his ladder, climbed up four rungs, fixed his eyes on an unsuspecting two by four and wailed down upon it preferring to shred the wood into chips on the floor. He would climb down, move the ladder three feet and ascend again to weaken his ardor and his arm on the ruins of the porch. He swung and sweated until his right arm grew tired. Then he readjusted his ladder to swing with his left. The off hand blows tended to miss their mark as often as they hit, but he did not care that he left marks in the wood he wanted to keep. All things worth their salt must endure some abuse.

As noon approached he flailed less at the house and settled into the slow steady rhythm of destruction. Now he would slide the claw down from the top behind the wood and push up with both of his hands to pry the pieces loose. The wood would groan at the nails that left oxidized circles in the cellulose and then crack into long jagged shards of board that Peter would finally pull down with a twist of his bare hand. When the wood was removed he would slide along quickly pulling the remaining nails with a quick rock of the hammer that would send the bent fasteners pinging down the rungs of the ladder.

Peter took a break to the kitchen to fill himself a glass of ice water and he shuffled slowly out the side door and around the lakeside of the house to gain some perspective distance on his demolition. He smiled a tired grin while he rubbed his exhausted shoulders and drank.
He did not even feel any hate for Doreen at the moment. Her curses were just a distant shadow at dusk blending in to the edge of an evil forest. All her prowling and preying demons seeped back deep into her bosky demeanor and stood fenced in shade. Peter stood far enough away now on the hilltop of a day's labor for it all to seem like a serene and enchanted landscape to be explored, but he had been there. To travel back to her now only would mean tearing through a thorn rimmed thicket with more blocked paths, uprooted trees, and swarming, blood sucking flies than all the forests of Michigan.

Peter stared at the broken eaves and the crumbling porch. He walked back into the kitchen to look at the boxes of his parents' past stacked around the table. He held up his left hand to look at the pale white flesh banding his third finger and said, "My work is here."

With that he grabbed a kitchen towel and mopped the sweat off his face and neck. He let himself cool and dry with his eyes closed before he allowed himself to do any heavy sifting. The boxes bore no discernible marks, but inside them manila folders with meticulously penned tabs stood organized by red ink. The first box's folders ran backwards on the tabs. The top folder read 1983 and the last 1964. Each was carefully crammed full of receipts and copies of tax forms. Each was the same red ink written in the cramped hand of his father. His father's scribbling in the margins interestingly added up a year's wage, subtracted expenses all in long hand on his own copies so that he could transfer the exact figures with unprecedented diligence and precision. Peter looked carefully at the digits that differed from his own. The ones that started at the top with a tiny hook, the fours whose cross brace arched elegantly bridging the space between the vertical lines all paled in Peter's memory to the sevens.

***

"Dad, why do you make your sevens that way?" asked a seventeen-year-old Peter. "You and Mr. Schenkelman."

"Who is Mr. Schenkelman?"

"My physics teacher. He writes his sevens just like you with the cross half-way down and the vertical line that runs straight down? They almost look like a backwards F. The whole class answered the same question wrong on the first quiz because we thought we were solving for another variable instead of looking at another number."

"Why does Mr. Schenkelman write his that way?"

"We asked him too."

"Well what did he say?"

"He didn't at first. He rolled up his sleeve and showed us a blue number on his forearm. It read A17778. All the sevens were crossed."

"Was he at Auschwitz, Peter?"

"How'd you know?"

Isaac looked up gravely from his forms and crawled into Peter's pupils with his melancholy sagging eyes. "I've known many who went to Auschwitz and few who survived. I've seen those tattoos, like brands on cattle. We were often herded together, naked in the cold. It was a terrible time of nightmares."

"It's funny."

"What could be funny about that?"

"I mean strange. Mr. Schenkelman said almost the same thing. He said, 'It was a time of nightmares in every waking hour.' He said that he wrote his sevens that way to remember the seventeen-thousand seven-hundred seventy–seven people who died before him and the seventeen-thousand seven-hundred seventy-seven people he wheeled across the compound."

"So many," seeped out of Isaac slowly like a leaking inner tube. His head was down and he focused on nothing.

"Mr. Schenkelman said that he actually counted the bodies he carried in a wheelbarrow where the Nazis commanded him to dump them in a mass grave they dug with heavy machinery. He said the graves were fifty feet wide, one-hundred feet long, twenty bodies deep and that he personally dumped seventeen-thousand seven-hundred seventy-seven in those holes. He said that he focused on the numbers to stay sane. He didn't count bodies, just numbers. He said one more and his number would have been up. Can you believe that dad?"

Isaac looked cold and said, "I'm often not sure what to believe."

"No one in class believed him. James Founder likes math puzzles and despises Mr. Schenkelman. He started scribbling on his scratch paper while Mr. Schenkelman was talking. When he started rolling down his sleeve James said, 'Mr. Schenkelman you're full of shit. If you carried four bodies per barrow load for five minutes a load it would have taken you more than three-hundred seventy hours to dump them. If you worked forty hours a week it would have taken more than nine weeks.'"

"Did Mr. Schenkelman punish James for such an outburst?"

"He usually sends James to the office, but he didn't that day. He just looked at James in a confused way almost like he pitied him. We felt uncomfortable and sat real quiet. Finally he said, 'We hadn't eaten. Eight could fit in a load and I did it in ten days.' Then he said it, 'It was a time of nightmares in every waking hour.' He made James pass out a homework sheet and sat in the corner for the rest of the hour and didn't speak to us again. We don't ask him questions like that anymore."

"It was the most horrible for those of us who lived because we never knew why we trudged on and thousands fell around us. I understand your Mr. Schinkelman. I too keep a sort of remembrance in my numbers."

"What do you remember, Dad?

"I remember to be careful."

"Careful of what? They're just numbers that doesn't look any more careful than my way, straight across and diagonally down."

Isaac looked nervously away from his small desk in the corner of the living room looking out for someone. He tore a piece of paper off a corner of the morning news he had not yet had time to read and picked up a black pen. "Peter, do you know the Hakenkreuz?"

"No, Dad," and Peter watched his father draw two jagged lines that intersected in the middle like some vile pin-wheel. "Oh, yeah the swastika, everybody knows that. Somebody carved it into Mr. Schenkelman's blackboard after he showed us his arm. He stood over James' physics book holding it closed with his fist for five minutes while he lectured the class on never using that symbol even as a joke because it belittled all humanity. James' ears were red for the rest of class, but at lunch he bragged how he had kept us from starting the new chapter on chaotic systems."

"Yes this swastika is a reminder to us all to be careful of those who promise too much and blame too few." Below his drawing Isaac wrote his seven now with his pen. "My seven, Peter, is a reminder to be careful. I will never again be destroyed by all the things this symbol represents," and with each word Isaac inked in an additional dark line to his number. With "Lust" he drew a vertical line up from the right side of the cross on the seven. With "Greed" he drew a vertical line down on the left side of the cross. When he spoke "Hate" running horizontally from the bottom of the number he created mirror image of the first swastika with a seven at its heart. "The Nazis always inscribed their statues and flags like the first swastika usually tipped up on a point like a diamond, but the way I draw it and what I remember in my sevens is the original meaning."

"I thought swastikas were always about evil. It looks so sinister in the movies swooping down on the sides of fighter planes. What is the original meaning?"

"It was a symbol of good luck – like lucky seven or a found penny. It is because of this that we must always be careful never to give away our power to those who will turn lies into truth, or those who will try to convince us that hell is a heaven. They made my country surrender their minds to evil laws and made us surrender our homes, our possessions, our families - our bodies in punishment while they swept across the land with their legal crimes."

"It doesn't make any sense. If they made the symbol so terrible and made you suffer so much, why do you write something that reminds you of it every day?"

"Because I am fortunate. Because they did not beat me – my mind or teach me to hate as they had. I arose from the flames of that with more love in my single heart than an entire Nazi nation that tried to kill me. I have you, your mother and a lifetime ahead of me to enjoy that those very people gave to me when they thought they had taken it away. I am taking back what they have stolen and making it my own." Isaac reached out with his right hand and placed it behind Peter's neck. He gently pulled him forward until their foreheads met. "You and my sevens always remind me how lucky I have been."

**

"What'd ya have on the first hole, Pete," said Tony Sciori with a knowing smirk drawing his lips across his face like a fish with a hook in his mouth.

"Seven." said Peter quickly.

82

Come Not To Us

"That's a helluva nice score on the first hole. You Three over is quite a feat considering you were in all four s never seen that done before. I mean I've been in the trap at dogleg and I've even seen my uncle pop from the first fairwa second, but you Pete. You were the first I've ever seen to go dead left into the greenside bunker, then blast out over the gree ...no the one on the right. He – he." chuckled Tony. "I'm surprised you didn't break seven clubs over your knee after that performance."

"Well they're not my clubs, so I'd better keep my cool." smiled Peter uncomfortably.

"Yeah rental clubs, they're great aren't they. I think you are the first guy ever to use that set since they opened this place. I swear I heard the cobwebs crack on the first tee when you pulled out your driver."

"Why'd we have to come to a private course? You know I have only played half a dozen times."

"What you want to play a round at the local munie with three foursomes stacked up on every hole watching you hit every goddamn trap between here and Lake Michigan? No my friend you better be glad your old pal can get you on here at Butterfield before most of the members climb out of bed. Besides the extra money for the greens fees should be worth it to you to keep down the number of witnesses to the massacre you've begun."

"Well why are we on the Red course? Aren't the White or Blue courses easier? Four-hundred yards for a par four seems like a little bit much to me for a starting hole."

"Hey, don't worry Pete the White course will be our second nine. Besides the only things that are going to be red after this round will be my score and your ass from me thumping it all the way around. I birdied the first by the way."

"Really, I think we should get together more. Our friendship really has a way of building me up."

Tony strode to the second tee and planted a spike in the ground long enough to hold down a tent in a hurricane. He took an easy practice swing that swiped the dew off the morning grass before he cracked a well placed fade on the right half of the fairway.

"Nice shot, Tony."

"Aw it's not as far as I'd like, but it'll work. I'll even make a prediction. Care to make a wager out of my prognostication since you won't play me straight up for anything?"

"Big word for an even bigger jackass."

"Hey, be nice to your host not many are invited here. We both guess my score and the closest wins a steak at the club restaurant."

"Alright, eighty-five."

Brett Ramseyer

"Surely you jest. I could guess eighty-four and be assured victory, ᴊt I'll make it interesting. In honor of 1969 in the year of our Lord in which we are blessed with this fine June day and in even more esteem to my favorite position –"

"Okay you pig, I've got it, three under par. Now quiet I'm about to out drive you." Peter waggled his forearms to relax, over swung and hooked his ball into a tree fifty yards down the fairway that kicked it farther into the woods.

"I wouldn't have put it that way," said Tony as he shouldered his bag, "But as you wish three under. Speaking of *under* how's your wife and my kid?"

"Why don't we skip the club restaurant and you can come to dinner at my place tonight. I'll buy the steak in thanks for the invite to the club and you can see how she is for yourself, with my attentive supervision of course. Besides you haven't been around since Michael was born."

"No I – I don't think I can make it tonight."

"What are you afraid of? We aren't a pair of farmers with a set of clippers ready to pull your pants down to domesticate you or something. You can be uncle playboy for five minutes, rock the baby and be out to a jazz club by nine to catch the next woman you'll teach to shoot three under par."

"Shows how much you know. Only a loser goes to a club before eleven."

"Well I'm sorry, I haven't been getting out much."

"Yeah, I'm surprised she let you out of the house. Shouldn't you be home wiping the babies butt or something."

"No, I'm out here so you can thump mine remember?"

"I'll come for a few minutes, but what if I shoot a seventy-seven?"

"Then we'll both count ourselves lucky. You can still come to dinner, but I'll make you pay for the steak."

14

With little notice late morning lumbered into early evening. Shade covered the east windows and sunlight peeked in the west. Piles of paper lay on every horizontal surface of the kitchen as Peter found his groove in organization. Tax forms and receipts spread across the table by year, newspaper clippings and magazine articles lined the hallway to the stairs, bond certificates and stock holdings stood lucratively on the counter, bank statements, mortgage payments, insurance policies, dry cleaning stubs, raffle tickets, Peter's grade school participation ribbons, shopping lists, check lists, work lists, all but Franz Liszt formed perfect rectangles all around the kitchen table where Peter played a theme and variation of hopscotch. Instead of throwing stones and picking them up he jumped and skipped on one and two feet building an ever greater court to deposit his father's lifetime string of monotony.

Isaac's horde of humdrum for the first time took flight in Peter's hands. The speed at which he doled these dull documents would have awed the greatest secretary and even impressed a circus crowd or two as he traveled about the room in a dance of distribution that literally left him slinging papers like Frisbees to land gently turning.

These blurred hours of spiraling paper made him forget the earlier concerns of the day. He did not look for the time until he reached for the final torn box where he began a few nights ago. The hands on the faceless clock ticked somewhere in the vicinity of five twenty and Peter began to think of his stomach that missed lunch and saw no dinner nearby. His enthusiasm enjoyed new energy as he grabbed the first handful of paper from the final box.

"I might as well push on through." Peter said to himself as he thought about how barren the refrigerator must be.

The least organized of all the boxes waited because he haphazardly tossed most of the contents back into it in the dark. It slackened the pace of his whirling dervish game, for now he resorted to reading more of the discombobulated mess to help it find its place.

For the most part his mother was right. Isaac hid his wealth well. He owned countless bonds and stocks that Peter could not possibly know the value of until he started researching the market. He even held two different whole life insurance policies that together equaled over one-hundred fifty-thousand dollars. Those pleasant shocks made him look again at the stocks. He hoped to see names like IBM, Xerox, and Apple, but they were far from household names and even further from recognizable words. The all looked like a collection of prefixes and suffixes without a root in sight. Names like INdeCon, Bi-med, and Privacor made Peter hope that they still existed so his mother could reap some benefit.

"Come on Dad be somewhat shrewd so I can bill Mom a tidy sum and not feel guilty."

Isaac stashed away no real fortune, but saved enough that Peter should see it brought home to Claudia. At least then she would pay more if not all of her bills and not feel so beholden to her son. Peter hoped that thought would brighten the melancholy that overwhelmed her since Isaac's death. He figured he should call her with the news of her modest fortune. He hoped he could ease her mind since she seemed so loathed to let these boxes of papers out of her sight and would certainly make a more cheery topic of conversation since he last called her. She would also like knowing that her money financed a successful search for buried treasure.

Peter with papers in hand skipped through his maze of organization to the phone. He lifted the receiver and dialed in tiny arcs eleven times to reach his mother. He released the phone onto his shoulder and brought it up to meet his ear. He took the small bunch of papers in both hands and continued to leaf through them and deposit them with a spinning flourish to their appropriate stack. Now he negotiated the long phone cord in his twirling work to look like a yo-yo traveling furiously up and down its string.

It took a multitude of rings before Claudia answered the phone sounding somewhat out of breath. "Hello, this is Claudia."

"Hey Ma – Peter."

"Peter, are you home? Doreen told me about the cottage."

"No, I'm hard at work sorting through Dad's stuff here at the cottage."

"Oh, well when are you coming home? It's been several days since that storm."

"Right now I'm not sure when. I've a lot of work up here to do. I'm doing a lot of demolition of the porch and clean-up right now. Today though, I've spent an entire afternoon going through these boxes."

"Don't feel you have to do it all at once dear."

"It's better this way, just to gut through it and find out what's here. I'm organizing it mostly so I can go back to what is important. I told you that a lot of this stuff was worthless. Dad kept a ton of things that could have been easily discarded –"

"You haven't thrown anything out!"

"Relax, Ma. It's all here. I know how sensitive you are about Dad's things."

"Well, it's just that I'm not even sure what is all there. What might seem like garbage to you could be a memento to me and your father."

"Maybe, but I've found out one thing for sure Ma."

Come Not To Us

"What is that?"

"Dad was pretty dull. I've seen dry cleaning stubs from 1958 and did you know that Dad had a work list that said he was planning to add two hundred square foot bedroom and bath to the old house. I think it was about the time he fashioned my makeshift room in the basement."

"He didn't spend much, did he?"

"It's paying off for you now, all that saving."

"What's left for me?"

"Life policies around one-hundred fifty thousand and some stock and bond certificates I don't know anything about yet."

"That doesn't sound so dull to me, Peter. I remember it all. The addition was supposed to be for an addition to our family, but it didn't work out."

"What? You lost a baby."

"In a manner of speaking, we were adopting you a brother."

"Really? Why adoption."

"We felt you needed a sibling and we could no longer conceive."

"Mom."

"Yes, Peter."

"Talking with you recently has made it seem as though a theater set has been caving in around me. You have a way of moving a piece of background off the stage and dropping a sandbag right on my head. I think I'm standing in the middle of a living room scene and I wake up lying in the middle of the street."

"Well, you were young and the child we picked died of pneumonia. After that your father said we should concentrate on raising you."

"So why didn't he build me the big addition instead of my cave," said Peter chuckling. He started shuffling one piece of paper after another quickly from the top of the pile in his hands to the back.

"He said he didn't want to spoil you," said Claudia and Peter could hear her smile for the first time in months.

"Maybe I should go through every piece of paper with you Mom and find out the whole story around our family."

"Knowing how much your father kept that could take years."

"Well that's how long we have to remember him." Peter looked down at his hands and picked a document off the top of the stack. "We could start now. This one's in German. It looks old and official. Was Dad the president of Germany before I was born?"

"Not even Burgermeister, son."

"Well this is close, let's see Ge – geburtsschein. Yeah, this says Geburtsschein."

Claudia giggled like an engine turning over once before dieing. "That's birth certificate. It has nothing to do with public office. There is no fortune hidden in Germany for you."

"That's too bad because my name is on here. Under Vorname it says 'Peter K.'. Then under Familienname it says 'Versteck'. That's you isn't it, Mom?"

Claudia hesitated before answering a quiet, "Yes. Versteck was my maiden name."

"Is this your brother or something? No, wait here's your name Claudia Maria Versteck under Mutter –"

"Peter I really don't –"

"Vater says unbekannt. Mom, what is unbekannt?"

"Peter my German is out of practice," flailed Claudia. "I'm tired. It's time to rest."

"Mom, I need your help. Who is this?"

"Good night, Peter," and the line clicked. Peter took the receiver and laid it on the kitchen table so he could hold the certificate in both hands. He scanned down through the ornate German text and tried to make sense of it.

Geburtsort: Augsburg. Mutter: Claudia Maria Versteck. Vater: unbekannt. Peter K. Versteck. 20 Juli. 1945.

***

It was July 20, 1951 and Peter spent all morning following Claudia through the kitchen as she put the finishing touches on a birthday luncheon for the family. She turned at a tug on her skirt and nearly toppled over her son.

"Mommy, where's Daddy?" Little Peter had illusions of his father putting the final pieces together on some magnificent present that he would wheel into the living room like a bike, go cart or scooter.

"He's picking up your aunt Clara and Wendell for your birthday party."

Peter's shoulders fell and he scrunched up his nose in a face it was better his mother did not see as she had a wet kitchen rag in her hand that could have straightened a dog's hind leg with the flick of a wrist and a crack. "Is he coming?"

"Who? Your father?"

"No, Wendell."

"What's the matter? Don't you like your cousin?"

"Only when he's away from me."

"Peter! I'd have your neck if it wasn't your birthday. No more. Be nice to Wendell. He'll be gone this evening. Oh, I hear them."

The hinges on the front door ground and a high pitched soprano baying turned circles around the rocking chair as Clara and Isaac closed the door behind them. Wendell continued to yelp like a scared hog before he stopped suddenly and sent a play arrow whistling by Peter's ear that stuck with a smack on the wall behind him.

"Well what a fierce little Indian you've turned out to be," said Claudia wiping her hands on her apron.

"I'm chief Tonto, me eat cake," shouted Wendell from underneath a fake feather headdress that fell down over his eyes. He pushed them up and pulled his second of three arrows over his shoulder from a leather quiver. "Cake now! Aunt Claudia or I'll have your scalp."

"Easy chief," said Isaac as he rustled the feathers on Wendell's head and pushed them down over his eyes again. "You'll have your cake and maybe some ice cream soon enough, then you and Peter can play the Lone Ranger and Tonto in the backyard."

"NO we can't!" said the little whelp who gave Indians a bad name. "He doesn't have a mask, a hat, a six shooter, or a silver bullet and where's his horse? I got all the fixin's for my birthday yesterday. Here's my bow, arrows and quiver. I can play the real Tonto."

"You forgot your headdress and moccasins," reminded Aunt Clara before Wendell began to tiptoe behind the furniture planning his next attack on Peter. He had designs on a game more like the Indian and the antelope than the Lone Ranger and Tonto. "I swear I spoil that boy too much. His father said I should just buy the bow and arrow, but the whole outfit looked just so cute in the store window and you should have seen him when he opened it yesterday. He's been whooping ever since."

Peter stood next to Isaac for a sense of protection and Aunt Clara bent down to look him square in the eye. "Well, how's it feel to be all grown up at five years old."

"How should he feel," answered Isaac "It's his birthday and he's a genius."

"Now Isaac," said Claudia with a note of trepidation and warning in her voice, "Don't make such outrageous claims."

"It isn't outrageous. He can already read, add and subtract. He'll be one of the greatest minds of our time. Clara, we're enrolling him in the first grade in the fall and skipping kindergarten entirely."

At this a strange silence came over the house as Wendell stopped whooping, tracking and shooting. He walked over and stood next to Peter who was only an inch taller than his four-year-old cousin. "He doesn't look so smart to me," he said looking his cousin up and down and nearly tickling his nose with the feathers. "Mom, I want to skip kindergarten and go into the first grade too," whined Wendell.

"I tell you what, dear," whispered Clara as she knelt down next to her son with her arm around his shoulder. "We'll let you skip school this year and you can start in kindergarten next fall. All right?"

Wendell thought for a moment and said, "Okay," before he tore through the kitchen toward the back door. He shouted behind him, "Come on bookworm. You play the teacher and I'll be the blood thirsty Injun about to slit your throat so's I can drag your girl by the hair back to my teepee!"

15

"I was born in 1946," said Peter as his forehead crunched down on the bridge of his nose. "Who is this?" He turned the dry parchment over to find some sort of direction for his thoughts on the back. He was only met with a random green pattern dyed into the paper. He wanted to call his mother back on the phone and demand some answers, but he doubted she would pick up the phone.

***

On the fifth ring Peter looked away from the mirror. He lost his focus on the three daubs of blood that hung in pregnant drips on his forehead. He called out from the bathroom in disgust. "Mom! The phone's ringing." His adolescent anguish rose while knocking the pale white swelling points off his blemished face. After ten rings he quickly wiped away the fresh drops and opened the door. "Are you going to get that?" he screamed down the hall.

After the eleventh ring an uneasy silence began to rise in Peter's mind and he began to hear the panicked liquid whoosh of his own heart through his ear drums. *What if it was for me? Janice calling.* He left a message with her mother who sounded rather annoyed with his call in the early afternoon. The clock now ticked past five and his senior prom loomed only two weeks, two hours and forty-five minutes away. *She said she was going to be at home all weekend.*

Peter walked into the living room where his mother sat pretending to read yesterday's paper. "Who was on the phone?"

"Your father."

"What did he have to say?"

"I don't know. I didn't pick it up."

"What? I'm expecting a call what if –"

"It was him."

"How do you know? This girl Janice is supposed to call me back today. It's really important."

"He always calls me back when I hang up on him."

"What are you two fighting about?" His relief let him sit on the sofa with one knee bent up under him. He would not have to call Janice yet to make sure she talked to him. *I'll put it off until eight – seven thirty – no eight.*

"We never fight, only disagree. Fighting is for fisticuffs. We never do more than argue. It will pass before Monday."

Brett Ramseyer

Peter looked at his mother with his eyes quite wide. "It's Saturday. Have you scheduled a disagreement for the whole weekend?"

"You know how your father is. When he's angry or hurt he broods. He walks out the door to be alone and to avoid who he's mad at."

"You?"

"Of course, you haven't seen him glower at you."

"I haven't seen him since breakfast. He didn't even say good morning."

"Sometimes the biggest arguments start before breakfast."

"What's the beef, Mom. Should I stay at a friend's house?"

"Certainly not, we don't want people talking besides it's all about the past. There isn't a thing to do about it all now."

"If it can't be changed then why is Dad so angry?"

"He wants me to talk about old times and I have had enough of them. I've put them behind me and he wants me to dredge up some war time filth. He says I need to 'Clear the air between you and me.'"

"Me? I wasn't born until after the war. I think you two should leave me out of it."

"Precisely, that is what I told Isaac. You don't want to be bothered with all our war baggage – shaved heads, starvation and all those depressing details."

"You've never told me those things."

"See, what teenage boy wants to hear that?"

"Actually it sounds pretty interesting. I've always thought of you and Dad as pretty boring. What's so terrible that Dad left?"

"Nothing of consequence – a letter."

"Uh-oh Mom. Is an old boyfriend looking for your American fortune?" said Peter grinning.

"Peter, park your tongue. I'm your mother," said Claudia reddening.

"Geesh, sorry. Well what was it?"

"As I've said, nothing. An old friend of mine," Peter began to smile. "A woman friend," straightened Cladia, "wrote to me to tell me that a Doctor I knew during the war has died."

"Did Dad really like him?"

"No."

"Did you?"

"I don't remember."

"But Dad wanted you to tell me about him?"

"Yes."

"That he died?"

"Yes."

Come Not To Us

"Was he famous or something? Dad loves history. Should I be learning about this guy for school?"

"I think not. His contributions to medicine were nefarious at best."

"Nefarious? What does that mean?"

"I guess I'm just trying to say that he isn't very important to us, Peter," said Claudia with a breathless exasperation.

"So why is Dad fighting with you about an unimportant man?"

"That's what I said."

"Dad, just wanted you to tell me?"

"Yes."

"Well you told me about him. Next time the phone rings you can answer it and tell him to come home."

"I could."

"Say Mom, speaking of the phone, can I call someone."

"Janice?" pried Claudia.

"I just need to use the phone."

"Fine, we all have our secrets. Oh, and Peter."

"Yes, Mom?"

"Be sure to buy her a nice corsage for your school dance."

***

"Flowers!? What the hell are you doing buying her flowers for?" argued Tony.

"I love her," replied Peter pointing to a bucket filled with baby's breath. "Three of those and some greens to round it out, would you please?" The clerk pulled the foliage up slapping the long stems on the side of the pail before laying them gently on a curling piece of white butcher paper. She turned away sliding open a refrigerated glass door.

"You said you wanted seven red roses?" asked the clerk.

"No, no. Seven *yellow* roses please."

"I'm serious. What is wrong with you? You're grinning and sappy. Where's the guy who mopes around eighty percent of the time so that I can crack a joke and help him pull his head out of his ass?" said Tony.

"He's hiding until Doreen breaks his heart."

"Why don't you just cut it out of your chest and put it on a platter? She knows she has you by the short hairs. Honesty like this will backfire on you soon enough."

"Tony, shut up. It's Valentine's Day and I am buying the woman I love some flowers. Then I'm going to walk over there, buy a little white card and a little white envelope and pour my heart out on six square inches. And I don't care if you, the clerk, Doreen or the whole world knows it."

"All right, fine, but why seven and why yellow?"

"Because it has been seven months since our first date, that you set up thank you very much, and she happens to adore yellow."

Brett Ramseyer

"Did you just use the word *adore?*"

"I did."

"Jesus Christ, I need *a door* to slam my head in. Come on Pete we're men. We don't use words like adore, cute, or glorious."

"I didn't use cute or glorious, but wouldn't this cute teddy bear make a glorious addition to my gift?"

"Hah! Ha-Hah!"

"I know. I'm funny when I'm happy."

"That wasn't laughter. I was dry heaving."

"Why are you here? You could be anywhere doing anything you want. Stop plaguing me. Go cuddle up with Ilene or a bus while you cross the street."

"Oh, Ilene and I are over. You're like three weeks behind."

"No wonder you're so grouchy." Peter pulled his wallet from his right rear pocket and laid a twenty on the counter that he drummed with his fingers. "I'm sorry she finally dumped you."

"Hey! Let's get one thing straight here, I broke it off with her. Tony Sciori doesn't get dumped."

"That's a good thing because look how angry you are when you're the one to end it." The clerk handed Peter his crinkling package. "Thanks." He and Tony walked underneath three clanging sleigh bells and into the street. They walked quickly toward the El and traversed a block and a half before Tony broke the silence.

"How could you not know that Ilene and I were over?"

"I haven't been around."

"Yet another reason I had to torture myself by coming with you on this trip. Somebody has to do the work in this friendship."

"You're right, but didn't a wise man once tell me, 'When faced with the choice of tux or tail, chose tail. Especially if she looks like she'll give you a chance to tuck your tail.'"

"That does sound wise. When did I say it?"

"At your cousin's wedding over winter break. Remember how you drove me there and then explained how you couldn't drive me back."

"I don't remember, but it sounds like me."

"That poor girl she was lucky you didn't kill her in an accident with as much as you drank."

"Oh yeah, Constance. I remember saying that now. She was the one who started making me think it was time to break up with Ilene."

"So why don't you buy her some flowers and cheer up."

"Connie? Please. I haven't seen her since I dropped her off at her door.

The two of them reached the steel stairs to the station and Tony bound up two steps at a time with his hands in the pockets of his leather jacket. Peter walked up slowly behind him carefully cradling his flowers. He stepped gingerly on his ascent as not to touch the icy rail that followed along at his side.

"She taught me another thing that night too," said Tony who stood square at the top of the stairs looking down at Peter. "The Big Bang Theory."

"You two contemplated the beginning of the universe?"

"In a manner of speaking although we didn't talk very much. It all has to do with energy. Massive amounts of energy gather together in two people getting closer and closer and closer until every fiber is so excited that there is nothing to do, but explode."

"I thought we were talking about astronomy, not sex."

"I am. I'm talking about all of it. It's nature. I'm talking about the stars, the planets, the sun, the moon, men and women. We're all part of a cosmic beginning. It's why the empty gesture of buying a girl flowers is so pitifully naïve and fruitless."

"You're just upset you're not having a Big Bang tonight. Leave me and my flowers alone."

"You never understand. I'm trying to help you. Every man and woman in a relationship comes to their Big Bang moment. For me and Constance it was quick, one night. With Ilene it built and died more slowly. With her it took from July to November, but it happened and it will always happen as long men and women function within the rules of the universe."

"You sure these aren't your rules?"

"Are you kidding? These came down from God. I'm just spreading his message in the hopes of helping my friend."

"You are a saint."

"Thank you. Now let me finish."

"Have I ever been able to stop you?"

"Of course not, because I accept the cosmic forces and flow with them. I cannot be stopped in my quest to educate. I'll be specific so there is no confusion. Ilene and I reached a point, a pinnacle, an apex, the quintessential biggest, best, most unbelievable bang I've ever known. I took her home for Thanksgiving and my parents went Christmas shopping on Friday. I stripped Ilene down in the living room. It was amazing. I can't even tell you, but I digress. I knew as soon as it was over that we would never replicate the experience again and we had reached our end. Just like the universe we had joined for a moment of explosion and just like all the planets and the galaxies we were left expanding away from each other at virtually the speed of light."

"And you figured all this out with Constance? What does this have to do with me and my flowers?"

"Oh Peter, I pity you. Don't you get it? Ilene and I were already far apart from each other. I was on another woman, on another planet ready to embark on another fatalistic explosion that would accelerate me farther from the girl I had fooled myself into thinking I loved. I had wasted December and part of January fighting the expansion of our relationship before I succumbed to the realization of the inevitable and broke it off. I'm telling you this to save yourself a lot of grief and a little money. You'd still have a twenty in your pocket if it weren't for you fighting nature."

"So you're telling me there is no such thing as love?"

Their train creaked to a deafening stop and the doors hissed open. Tony walked on and grabbed a pole overhead.

"Exactly," said Tony, "That's why all relationships are doomed because it is all a matter of who wises up first. Whoever finds out second might as well have died in the explosion."

16

Peter collapsed in bed with a headache and awoke with heartburn. Not the kind that burst in the mouth like a volcanic mix of last night's dinner and acid, instead it pressed down on his chest constricting his ribs and smoldering his pumping muscle. In his dream he fought open his pants and groped for someone soft and round. Someone also branded his chest in slow motion. He could feel the glowing iron descend superheating the air around it. His hair melted into acrid fumes and his flesh boiled before it reached him. Still, he probed forward to sink sweetly into ecstasy only to recoil in the diametrical agony of the iron crushing his ribs and cooling itself ever so slowly in him.

He looked down at his torment where he blew the white wisps of steam away from his face like a hero cooling the barrel of his pistol. Stuck in the center of his being lay embedded forever the diamond edged symbol of Nazi Germany. His eyes widened and he held his breath stifling a scream to look below his waist. His eyes traveled from the bristled union, around a navel shaded by undulating breasts. There a swan white neck that arched gracefully away from him in a back dive that hid the face of his lover. Hovering in the haze of dark and light, two hands clutched the shaft of the branding iron. The interlocked fingers linked over tendon twitching arms that seemed to grow out of his mother's grisly visage.

This burning pressure made Peter bolt upright from a turbulent night. He exhaled loudly and began to breathe rapidly through his mouth to slow his heart rate. His right hand reached for his sternum and clawed briskly through nothing, but his own soft pectorals.

He shook his head once and swung his feet to the floor. He stood up naked, grabbed a pair of paint stained khaki shorts and pulled them up over his waist. He slipped his sockless feet into the soft leather of some high topped work boots and shuffled out to the reemerging porch before he bent down to seize the gold and brown laces and flip them around the brass hooks that lined his ankle. He battened them down tightly and began to work without a shirt or breakfast. He hoped to silence his thoughts in the din of jagged blades spinning through pine and the crisp whacks of his hammer loosening the galvanized coating off of broad headed nails.

He abandoned the idea of another sun porch and worked on an extension of the living room with a sliding glass door and windows that faced out toward the lake. He decided to leave the wall between him and the VanDuinen's solid with not so much as a knothole in it for Rita to look through.

Brett Ramseyer

The morning started cool and very crisp. Peter spent the first hour rubbing and cleaning razor blade-like crust out of his nostrils with his thumb. By eleven a sultry breeze had worked its way northwest of off Little Point Sable and nestled a lake full of moisture in the middle of the bosom of West Michigan.

Peter worked through lunch until sweat ran into his eyes. He left the kitchen and its maze of papers in solace and raised the pale yellow skeleton of walls on all three sides. He stopped only long enough to walk to the edge of the lawn and submerge his head in Pentwater Lake from his short section of dock. He opened his eyes under water and watched the living breathing particles cast a verdant brown glow over the sun beating down through the cloudless haze. He straightened his neck and slicked his dripping hair back over his head. He lowered his lips and drank deeply for two minutes feeling his pores fill back up from the inside. With such a flotilla of sediment and seaweed he figured that such a long drink offered the nutrition of a salad and he rose from his knees. He wiped his mouth with the back of his hand that left tiny white scratch marks across his skin from his salt and pepper beard he had neglected for a week.

Reinvigorated he set back to the slow work climbing a ladder, measuring angles, and setting a roofline. Before he could even traverse half the width of the house setting two by fours Bill came around the corner.

"Well neighbor you've been busy."

"Morning Bill," mumbled Peter around lips full of nails.

"More like evening, you mean."

"Is it that late already. I've been working since dawn."

"It's coming nigh on six o'clock. The Mrs. asked me to invite you to supper if you are so inclined."

"Oh thanks Bill, but I've been working all day. It makes a man proud to work a full day. I'd just as soon push on until dark if you don't mind."

"Suit yourself, but I'll wager that Rita will be over here with a warm plate soon enough." He turned and picked his way across the yard strewn with lumber. "I'm glad to see you rebuilding."

"It seemed like the right thing to do."

"Well, I'll see you around the neighborhood," and Bill disappeared around the corner of the house.

Peter climbed down his ladder and wiped his face with a greasy towel that lay on an old T.V. tray. He began to think of Rita coming over with an aluminum foil covered plate and he started to feel queasy. He belched a dry empty knot out of his stomach and ducked into the living room. He snatched a white t-shirt piled up on the couch as a pillow and slid into it. He removed his keys from a hook in the hall and exited out the lakeside. He walked under the trees on the east side of the house, circled around to the front of the garage and drove off for supper.

Peter stuck to the scalding leather seats of his Mercedes and moved his hands around the steering wheel quickly to try to keep them cool. It was easy to do around the endlessly winding road that nearly switched back over and around the forested dune. The road meandered at the lapping water's edge, turned abruptly away, rolled over slopes and clung to bramble covered cliffs that surrounded tiny coves all in less than a mile of driving. He broke out into the light on Longbridge and came to a stop in the center of his lane. His turn signal ticked to the left and he waited for a car to pass that headed into town. The driver and his wife cruised forty-five in no particular hurry, but Peter could see them smartly dressed with two more adults in the backseat. He looked down and his dust covered arms still holding beads of sweat around the base of his hair follicles and he turned sharply right behind a rusted red pick-up.

He followed the driver out under the highway to Old 31. They both turned north onto a flat plain past a motel in a latter stage of decay brought on by the interstate bypass two miles away. Peter almost hoped to follow this driver home for an invitation to a meal with his wife and dirty footed kids, crammed in a single-wide's kitchen where the linoleum curled up before it met the cabinets.

The pick-up slowed over a bridge and turned right without signaling. A trail of blue smoke poured out the tail pipe as he accelerated. The pale fog obscured the path to poverty that Peter entered as he put more pavement between himself and the lake. A half mile more and the truck merged off onto the shoulder and slowed onto a dusty lot between the road and a squat white building protected by expanses of stout green pipe and two cracked railroad ties that stood planted on end in the ground. A length of dark wood stretched between them. Its green lettering echoed the stark white block letters screwed into the shingles of the narrow roofline. MURPHY'S sandwiched there between two green shamrocks.

The amalgam of additions and after thoughts tied together on the side of the road. The main cinder block structure crouched under a false front roof of green asphalt shingles. They tried to hide the pipes and vents that spewed the aroma of grease, stale beer and cigarette smoke out into the foliage of a dense forest encroaching on the building. It hid various flat roof lines that came over the decades of modest expansion. Stretching from the right of the building a white steel sided space with a steel roof painted silver halted the rusted truck among the five other cars already parked. By the time Peter stopped up next to the right of the truck and stepped out of his Mercedes the final creaks and groans wobbled out of the pick-ups body. Peter closed his door and spun to a grease ringed fingernail pointing over the bed of the truck.

Brett Ramseyer

"You foll'n' me?" accused the rusty pick-up driver.

"No – I'm hungry. They've got something to eat here haven't they?"

"Yeah, they got good eats for a hole at the edge of the wilderness. What's it to ya?"

"Dinner I suppose," shrugged Peter too tired and hungry to be intimidated. He walked around the front of the pick-up and into the door. The man stood dumbfounded for a second outside at how easily he was dismissed. With nothing to do he dropped his finger and headed into the tavern. He walked in and blinked rapidly waiting for his eyes to adjust to the dark interior. The vertical wood paneling slurped up the meager light that dribbled around the edges of the only two windows of the place. The driver stood in the doorway and looked to his left across the bar. He panned across the cheap laminate tables with red vinyl cushioned chairs all the way to his right over the juke box into the addition with the pool table. He could not find the stranger from the Mercedes. He set his hands on his hips and mumbled.

From behind the bar overpowering the tin sounding speakers of the television rang a loud voice. "WE ALREADY HAVE A DOOR JIMMY. GET THE HELL OUT OF THE WAY!"

He turned half smiling and shot back, "Cool it Phyllis. Did somebody just come in here?"

"Maybe. Maybe not," Phyllis replied over the top of a frothing pint.

"Fine. Be of some value and pull me a draft. I've got to drain the main vein."

"Just go Jimmy. Nobody wants you to announce every time you break wind."

An old white haired man growing off the corner stool of the bar like a mushroom wheezed out a chuckle before tilting his head back and tossing in a peanut. He crunched down and his pink drunk cheeks turned scarlet before he sputtered out a series of coughs that he quelled by draining half of his long neck.

"Old bitch," muttered Jimmy as he kicked open the men's door. He unzipped while he walked and watered down the wall of the urinal. He started reading the faux marble paneling on the divider that read like a *Hustler* comic strip with swelling body parts replete with curling hair, measurements, and ownership labels. Many still questioned their authenticity with vulgar scribbles of their own. He read between the urinals: *For a gOOd time call Dawn 873-36 double D.* He started to smile at what he wrote when the stall door next to him opened and he saw the driver of the Mercedes walk over to the sink to wash his hands.

"You better watch your back in a place like this," called Jimmy over his shoulder.

100

Come Not To Us

"Don't worry. I had a friend who taught me to sit where I could watch all the doors," said Peter as he wiped his hands on white paper towel. He reached up with the towel as a barrier to the handle on the door backed by a black splotch caused by years of unwashed hands. He held the door open with his foot and shot the wad of wet tissue at the can along side the sink.

Peter escaped notice on his direct route entrance to the bathroom, but upon his exit Phyllis called out, "Can I help you?" before he'd made three steps toward the bar. Peter bellied up and picked up a folded blue menu wedged in a rack of condiments.

He scanned through list of deep fried this and deeper fried that before he looked up. "I'll have a beer to start."

"That's why we're here," said Phyllis pulling back on a tab marked *Beer* written in permanent marker.

Peter walked to the last stool at the end of the bar closest to the window and sat down. Phyllis, a large women shaped much like a giant grape with appendages sticking out at even intervals stepped half way down to Peter and slid the glass down to him. "That'll be two bucks," she said forcing a half smile that revealed a meandering row of gaped teeth rimmed with brownish-yellow enamel stained from years of smoking unfiltered cigarettes.

"Can you just run me a tab? I'll have a quarter-pounder too please."

"You want that as a basket?"

"Sure, and a side of mushrooms."

She scratched on a pad and turned away. "The works on the burger?"

"Yeah."

The day's work took its toll on Peter and the mist of fat that circulated out the swinging kitchen door flooded his mouth with spit. He wrapped his hand around the slippery glass and emptied the beer before he set it down. He started to look around and read the motto of there being more old drunks than old doctors and understood why they planted so many thick barricades between the road and the tavern. *They must have had a bout of late night drive-ins that they decided to stop just outside the windows so that the patrons would have something vaguely interesting to look at.*

Peter watched the red truck driver pick-up his beer. Jimmy glared sideways at Peter and swaggered into the pool table where two working class men in dirty jeans and block pattern shirts with their sleeves rolled up past their elbows played nine ball. Jimmy slapped his quarters on the rail of the table and called out, "I got winner." Then Peter turned away, oblivious to the men frittering the week's pay.

Phyllis returned from the kitchen and another full headed beer had already appeared in front of Peter. He lifted it and said, "Thanks." Phyllis nodded without looking up. She turned and slid the chrome door of a black Perlick refrigerator open. She bent down inside and pulled out a long brown bottle. She reached over to the right of the refrigerator and with a flip of her wrist the beer coughed open and she set it down in front of the red-faced mushroom at the end of the bar.

He said, "Phyllis, you're a mind reader."

"Yeah, I'm a real fortune teller. Your mind's been writing the same thing for fifty years."

"Even so, if my wife would only die I'd marry you tomorrow."

"Not a chance old man. You'd get your own beer at home."

"Then forget it."

"Good. The engagements off."

Peter still thirsty emptied half his beer before he felt his empty stomach pulsating around his ale. Soon his eyes followed suit, but he finished before Phyllis waddled back from the kitchen and set his food in front of him. She came back with some ketchup, refilled his glass and left him alone.

The burger went first, the mushrooms, the beer and then the fries. A car salesman shouted, "Low, low, low!" from the television set in the corner. The men who trickled through the door filled the bar and tried to hide the room in a screen of smoke. The late comers slowly filled the tables trailing away from the bar. They stomped in clean, dirty, short and tall. They talked about machinery and bumpers and several showed the intricacies of their day's work by extending a thumb upward and thrusting it up into their other fist like a ball into a hitch.

Someone flipped through the selections on the juke box and cranked it up. Peter did not know the tune, but he felt sure the musicians knew how to put the honky in front of tonk. The singer twanged about his full-shirted girl when she slipped from the kitchen over to Peter and leaned toward him from behind the bar. Her white ribbed tank top strained against her breasts that pushed full over Peter's basket. He found himself wiping the corner of his mouth with the back of his hand.

"How do they taste?" she said.

"Sorry, what?" stammered Peter as his head rose reluctantly to a familiar face.

"Your fries."

"Oh, ah great. Sorry," he smiled. "I was looking- "

"At my tits?"

Peter blushed violently. "They *were* next to my side of fries."

"Yeah, I was looking for a big *tip*. You wouldn't know anyone who could help me with that would ya?" said Dawn from under the crooked smile that Peter remembered from the road. "You look different with a beard."

Come Not To Us

Peter rubbed his cheeks up and down with his thumb and fingers. "I've been working a lot. I haven't thought to shave."

"Don't worry. I like it. It takes the pretty boy off your chin. Makes ya look more like a man."

Peter brought his glass to his mouth for something to do and brought it back down to the bar. She delicately placed her hand on top of his and said, "Let me put a head on that for ya." She winked and slid her fingers down the tab while she grinned back at Peter. Warmth built from the inside out and he liked his flirtatious mood.

She came back and assumed her provocative position inviting his stare. "My name's Dawn. I meant to tell ya when you were stuck in the mud, but my neighbor seemed a little to eager to help."

"I'm Peter. You don't like Dale?"

"Let's just say I don't like bein' looked down on."

"Well, I'm looking down and the view isn't half bad," said Peter before the sharp crack of a mug on the bar startled him.

"Is this tourist, botherin' you Dawn," sneered Jimmy with a dented pool cue in his hand.

Dawn stood up and tugged her top up from the tank straps. "Does it look like I'm bothered Jimmy Lee?"

"Well I'm pretty bothered," said Jimmy looking at Peter the whole time. "I'm tired of city boys comin' into our nice places and stinkin' them up."

Dawn grabbed his mug off the counter and filled it quickly. "The only thing stinkin' in here is you Jimmy. Christ, I could smell that pig farm on you while I was in the back washin' dishes. Go play some pool over there so's at least the smoke has the chance to fight the stench of shit on ya."

Jimmy set his tongue in his cheek and looked at Dawn. Then he looked back at Peter and wagged his inky finger at him. "Just be warned. I don't want to see you in here again y'hear?"

"Jimmy git the hell away from me before I tell Phyllis you're threatenin' payin' customers and she breaks that cue over your stupid ass head."

Jimmy huffed and dropped his shoulders and walked away, but Dawn kept an eye to him across the room while he gesticulated to the men playing pool and pointing across the tavern. She tended the other side of the bar for a time before walking back to Peter.

"Listen. It's nearly eight. Why don'tcha settle up. I been on since noon and Phyllis owes me a favor. I need to git outta here. You mind givin' me a ride home?"

"I'll give you a ride," said Peter and he tossed a crumpled twenty on the bar and slipped out the door while Jimmy Lee concentrated on a shot with the bridge. Dawn walked out the back and was already waiting on the passenger side of Peter's car.

"I remembered your car."

"Only Mercedes in the lot. It's open."

17

"Can't this car go any faster?" asked Dawn twenty seconds after Peter turned onto Old 31.

"I'm four pints into a coma. You want to go there with me?" replied Peter. "My eyes are already glazed over. I don't think I should be driving."

"Shoot. Four is just when I start feeling good. I should have grabbed a couple for the road, but I didn't think of it. If you're worried, just drive real slow. I know a place close that we can set for a bit for you to sober up."

"I'm game. It isn't even dark yet."

"Turn right," Dawn commanded.

Peter leaned in and rounded the turn back toward the cottage and the two drove in awkward silence until they passed under the highway.

"It's just past the fruit stand on the left," she said craning her neck and leaning forward to look around the rearview mirror. "There it is. You see?"

"A barn?"

The River Barn stood like an old time fort daring the enemy to attack. Facing the road, a simple solid red wall rose three stories out of a knoll. They passed it slowly and Dawn said, "Turn here." Peter picked out a lonely two-track that cut through waving waist high grass. "Pull around back and stop," she finished in her navigation. The car steered itself around the curling dusty bands that circled behind the building and moved up a surprisingly steep slope hidden from the road. Peter parked on the incline and set the brake. "We're here," said Dawn as she opened the door and sprung from inside.

The centennial barn set on a small bluff overlooking the flood plain of the Pentwater River and the beginnings of Pentwater Lake. From where they stood civilization disappeared. To the south and west willows wept up out of the moist silt river banks and cascaded limply down toward the clearing. Peter felt as if they landed a canoe with Father Marquette a few yards away and walked behind the shadow of this old barn. If not for the inconsistent hum of cars speeding past, the two of them could swear they traveled to a simpler time.

Peter looked up at the abandoned structure that appeared strong enough to withstand another century. On the second story toward the lake laths set wide apart allowed light to pour into the depths. Window openings covered in red wire mesh took the place where not a single pane of glass hung. Peter walked up the hill to a small hinged door. The bottom stood away from the jam while a padlock held the middle shut through a twisted metal latch. The latch, the lock, the door, the hinges were all painted inadequately red in someone's haste to cover the building. Peter crept up and peered into the basement where the dirt floor sloped with the grade of the hill. Overturned barrels, pipes and empty pallets leaned against each other in the powder dry dust. The foundation constructed of hundreds of Michigan stones peppered the base with colors: red, gray, golden brown or black with streaks of shimmering white quartz. Each no bigger than a cantaloupe once swung in the palms of a strong man who carried two at a time to set them firmly in the concrete that now looked more like grains of sand clinging together with spit.

"Come on," summoned Dawn as she circled from behind Peter and grabbed him by the hand, "This way."

Peter followed the hot pressure of her hand up the rest of the slope and to the level of the second story. "I've driven by here hundreds of times," he said, "But I've never really looked at this."

"That's what we counted on in high school," she said as she tugged Peter toward a small hinged door a third of the way down the east wall of the barn. "The rich kids partied in the Plains or at their parent's lake house if they left town, but my friends and I came here."

"Isn't this a little too close to the road?"

"Naw, it's a busy enough road that no old retirees will complain about a few cars going by and you can't see any houses from here." She released Peter's hand to reach for a piece of rusted wire threaded through the latch and twisted half a dozen times. She pulled it apart quickly and waved him inside.

Thirty feet above the ceiling rose to an obtuse point supported by hundreds of four inch trunks felled in their straight adolescence. They split down the middle to create a smooth surface on which to tack the deck of the roof. Most retained their scarred bark clinging to them, but below rose full grown timbers twelve by twelve inches thick stripped down to dry bone. These stout legs grew out of the floorboards and spread into massive arms pushing outward on the walls. They spoke of might and will that its two visitors did not possess.

The setting sun streamed in through every knothole, crack and window of the west wall. The light reflected off floating insects and perpetually circulating dust to cast a golden glow around the open loft. It looked like a church under a heavy storm when the sun breaks behind the altar and fills the nave with fantastic light through a stain glass window.

"The best place is up here," said Dawn setting one foot on a peg and reaching up a staunch post. She climbed to the beam and swung herself with a surprisingly graceful dexterity twelve feet above the floor to sit. She scootched her butt over with her hands at her sides and patted the dust covered place next to her.

"I'm drunk remember."

"Best time to try it, Peter, it won't hurt if you fall."

He gingerly put his foot on the first peg and felt like a lineman scaling up to high voltage wire. When he reached the beam he lurched up and came down heavily on his stomach over the beam. He groaned out a lung full and slowly turned to a sitting position.

"What the hell are we doing here?" he asked.

"Waiting for sunset."

Peter crinkled his nose and looked at the wall between them and the sun. "Okay, you're the local. I'll wait and see. I take it you came here a lot."

"Enough. We didn't always drink you know."

"You had sex too."

"If the company was good," she smiled.

"It really wasn't like all that. Sometimes we'd just come to run away."

"Who?"

"Me and my little brother."

"Did you live nearby?"

"No, we lived where I live now."

"That's quite a few miles to run."

"I'd drive Dad's truck."

"What were you running from?"

"Dad."

"Not a nice guy then?"

"No."

"I was lucky. My Dad was good. I don't think I ever ran from him."

"He must not a drank."

"No he didn't. He told me once he'd lived too many nightmares to be out of his head anymore.

"He sounds smart."

"He was. I miss him."

"Dead?"

"Last year. I didn't go in to see his body. I just stared at an arrangement of red and white carnations tied with a black ribbon. They closed his casket and lowered him in the ground before I realized I should have looked."

"Did he love you?"

"Yes."

"That's all you need to know."

"I guess it is," said Peter.

They sat quietly for a minute. Dawn inspected the lines fanning out from Peter's eyes. She decided something with a long drawn breath. She began to speak, but only after looking away toward the sunlit wall. "I didn't look at my Dad's body either. He died this year. He was a piece of shit, so I didn't have a funeral. I had the county send him off for science. I figured if they cut him up and looked inside they could figure out what was wrong so they could keep other people from being like him." She looked at Peter and smiled weakly. "All I got back from 'em was a white box of ashes in the mail. Can you believe that? Right through the mail like a package of cookies. I got excited at first, thought it was somethin' I ordered that I'd forgotten about. I opened it up, but the letter inside just said, 'Human Remains.' I know'd what it was then. I read the rest of the letter careful. I thought it'd say what they found in him."

"Did it?"

"Naw. There was a phone number, but I didn't call. Maybe whatever was wrong just burnt up in him before it spread."

"What'd you do with him?" asked Peter.

"The ashes?" Peter nodded. "Let's just say I flushed him right where he always belonged."

"We are lonely sort of people, Dawn."

"We don't have to be tonight," she said putting her hand halfway up Peter's thigh. She inched closer and put her head on his shoulder. She looked at the wall that already started to fade from a gold to an orange aura. "I remember one time we came here. Dad was workin' second shift at the canning factory. He came home at two in the mornin' drunk as hell. I woke up to my little brother screamin'. Dad was thumpin' him like I'd never seen. I jumped between 'em and pushed my brother out into the hallway. Dad said, 'Oh you want to be alone, huh?'" She stopped and swallowed.

"When he was done he told me I was the worst lay he'd ever had. I cried and ran out the door with my brother. I stole Dad's keys and his money clip. We drove here and stayed for a week until the sheriff found me in town buyin' food and he made me go home because Dad had called him."

"I'm sorry," was all Peter could think to say. He put his left hand around her and held her tightly under her arm.

"No matter. That's how I know the sunsets here are good. Me an' my brother'd watch 'em right here. It'll turn pink last," she said and it did. In the soft glow she turned her head and buried her lips in Peter's neck. She planted soft wet kisses in the furrows of his beard. He reached farther around her cultivating a hillock with his fingers and together they raised a fruitless crop to feed their loneliness.

Dawn moved first. She curled lithely around the post as she slid silently to the barn floor. Peter fixed his gaze on the steady rise and fall of

Come Not To Us

her billowing chest as he descended purposefully. Beer coursed through his veins, an elixir of inhibition, and his wife never crossed his mind.

Backing away from Peter one foot behind the other Dawn's hips swayed seductively on top of a white six-paneled door that stretched out between two distressed and wobbling saw horses. The knob, latch and hinges had all been removed and played the table for their banquet of adultery. She welcomed him in and wrapped her ankles behind his knees. They struggled through each others pale mantles to nuzzle close to the pink underneath.

Peter stood with his hands clasped behind of the small of her back bracing her up. With her hands gripping his arms she looked into his dark serious eyes and shut her own. She lifted her limbs over her head together and she dove in an arch backwards over Peter's hands. She gave over to his control and the last rays of light glinted off her moist neck.

Outside tree frogs raised their chorus of whistles to summon the faint buzz to the meal. Transparent wings and filament legs rose out of the cattails, floating like feathered seeds to silently disappear in evening's insatiable mouths. Humidity spread over the marshland, the air hung absolutely still waiting for morning's cool dense fog.

Brett Ramseyer

18

!!PILGRIM!!

Peter stood with a purpose. The sign overhead mocked him again just as he knew the old German would. His eyes would spill over and no news would rain hard enough to wipe the scarred smile off the twisted skull that protruded from his body. Yet, Peter stood, a pilgrim, in an unholy land seeking chastisement for the void in his chest that seemed more vast than when he stumbled into the glow of his headlights to end his suffering.

Today he harbored no thoughts of suicide. He sheathed no gun, no knife, no stick in his pocket to jumble his insides. He feared no mocking or intimidation. He reveled in the pure predatory joy a cat feels in tormenting a mouse.

COME NOT TO US

He read the phrase and batted it around playfully between his paws.

GO HOME AND MAKE

SOMEONE ELSE HAPPY

That he pinned down by the neck and nonchalantly looked around his surroundings. A yawn feigning boredom and admitting a long night escaped into the morning. He knew Doreen did not pine away for him at home.

OTTO AND ANNA

Their names made the final futile attempt to stave off any visit with a silent squeak and Peter set off down the two track driveway that curved between two overgrown crabapple trees in full spring flower. Their sweet fragrance made a perfect appetizer. He licked his lips in anticipation for when he would behold his prey and crunch satisfactorily down on his skull with his mere Jewish presence.

As he passed an ancient red water pump hidden in a stand of trees next to the house whose rusted handle had never coaxed a drop from the ground he heard his plaything. The melodious clink of aged barkless maple rang through this tiny valley. Otto stood thirty yards farther down the path tossing small logs into a wheelbarrow for his wood burning stove.

"Morning Otto!" Peter shouted as he continued to stride forward.

The old man turned partly before he continued his morning chore with the toss of half a dozen more logs. "You are just in time. Vheel dhose nach Hause, bitte. I vill consider it payment for zhe dings you vant me zu translate."

Peter stopped for a moment remembering the Gerburtsschein. He lifted the barrow handles and then felt the burden of his life back on him. His visions of feline superiority slipped away in the shuffle of the two men's feet.

"I didn't come to have anything translated," said Peter unconvincingly

"Oh den, you have only come zu beat an old man for shport." The skin under Otto's eyes were still dark near the nose and yellowing out around the edges.

"No, no beating," and Peter hung his head. "I'm sorry. I shouldn't have let you anger me."

"Ach, I vas glad zu see you could be."

Otto motioned for Peter to pick up a piece of canvas with two loops for handles. Peter laid it in the wheelbarrow and stacked the links in it while Otto went ahead into the house. What took the old man several minutes to toss in the barrow took Peter thirty seconds to load into the carrier and bring into the kitchen.

"It ist zu hot für Kaffee. Vould you like Kuchen?" said Otto as he lifted an overturned bowl off a plate with three pieces of cake.

"I would," said Peter whose empty stomach began to remind him this was the second day in a row without much to eat. Otto slipped a fork under one of the pieces and shakily transferred it to a small saucer. Another he picked up with his fingers and began to eat. The other he pushed along the counter to Peter.

"I guess I do have one thing for you to translate."

"Do I need my glasses?"

"No, I didn't bring it. It is only a few words. Are you familiar with Geburtsschein?"

"Ja, auf Englisch sagt man birth certificate."

"And Vater is father, right?"

"Naturlich."

"But what is unbekannt?"

"Unknown."

Peter sat puzzling over 'unknown' with his tongue pressing frosting against the roof of his mouth.

Come Not To Us

"Yours sounds like the zhe certificate of a promiscuous Mutter," interrupted Otto. "In some vays it ist safer not zu know your Vater, but you miss on zhe learning.

"I knew my father."

"Dis hauling of vood reminds me of an important lesson he taught me. It vas a black belted lesson dat on zhe kitchen hook hung."

"My father never beat me."

"Ja, und you've been scared all your life. Mit mein older Bruder Alois gone, I vas zhe oldest boy at seven. I feared mein Vater at first, den vun day he tore zhe hook from zhe vall und pinned me next zu a glowing stove für allowing the vinter vind zu blow zhe door open. I had tried zu haul a load of vood zu large für mein arms und had not been able zu shut zhe door. It vas a tirty minute lesson. After ten minutes I prayed to Gott für Vater zu shtop, after tventy minutes I cried and begged him zu shtop, after tirty minutes I vaited qvietly knowing Vater ruled me und vould kill me. He had not spoken zhe entire time, he only flogged. Wenn I qvieted only zhe vood in zhe stove popped vile mein Bruder Edmund hid behind meine Mutter. Only den did Vater shtop. He shtood over me und said, 'Ask your Mutter für somzing to eat.'"

"God, you must have hated the bastard."

"Ja, he vas a bastard, but on zhe contrary I never loved him more dann zhat day."

"Why? He beat you. How could you love that?"

"All people remember wenn power held zhem, controlled zhem, und cared für zhem. Mein Vater vas right. Zhe wind was cold und I vas hungry. You see. He kept me varm, fed und taught me zhe correct vay zu hold power und I have not been frightened since zhat day."

"He never apologized?"

"Nein! Only zhe veak apologize! It vas I who apologized zu him und countless ozers who later apologized zu me. Look at you. I had a shtick und you had zhe Luger, but it vas you who came back zhe next day zu apologize zu me." Shtrong eqvals right und veak eqvals wrong. It ist a directly proportional eqvation."

"Might doesn't make right."

"You and Lincoln may agree, but you both assume Gott cares.

"God doesn't care?"

"Not any more."

"So he wouldn't care if I cheated on my wife?"

"Nein. I built a guest house für zhat alone."

"He wouldn't care to see me wake up in some poor woman's trailer to the bulging eyes of her troll like daughter staring down at the strange man in her mommy's bed?"

"It vould not even cause a flutter of his shleeping eyelids. Komm. I vill show you."

"What? God sleeping?"

The old man shuffled away from the dining nook to the front door. He lifted a red flannel lined jacket off a peg. Peter embarrassed at the struggling pace offered to help.

***

"May I take your jacket," asked Peter, as Tony Sciori stepped into the cramped foyer. A few clumps of pristine flakes melted on the black leather shoulders.

"Sure Pete, there's plenty of body heat trapped in here already. Jesus. I didn't know you knew this many people let alone have this many like you enough to show up at your place on New Year's Eve."

"It's amazing how much more popular I've become in three years married to a beautiful woman."

"You don't say? Where is the mistress of the house?" Tony stood on his toes and straightened his spine to peer over the flocks of flowing hair shining in the living room.

The buzz of party introductions and patter of flirtatious laughter gave an undulating bass line to the chime of ice bobbing in scotch glasses. As the night grew the volume went the way of the champagne bubbles. Peter smiled in the midst of it with his friend.

"She's in the kitchen probably – hey speaking of beautiful," said Peter.

"Tony you made it," said Doreen dancing her way through the tight throng of guests. She held above her head a sloshing bowl at the end of each lithe, bare arm. Her wriggling hips and twisting torso drew the admiration of both men's eyes like a Fitzgerald flapper shimmying at a Long Island gala. "Where's your date?" she asked kissing past each of Tony's cheeks in the cosmopolitan air of a hostess running the coolest party in town.

"Oh no, no dates tonight. It's easier this way. No explaining to do in the morning."

Doreen crossed her arms in front of her in the final flourish of her fandango offering up the bowls to the two men. "What are we drinking?" asked Peter.

"Gin and tonic, boys."

"Here's to no explaining," toasted Peter.

"No explaining," echoed Tony. He pounded it down and twirled the bowl on his middle finger. "In the spirit of our toast Mrs. Sonderling your exquisite grace awards sufficient explanation to my need for a dance. You look like just the piece of luck I need to lure one of these lovely ladies out from a corner."

"There's no music," she cautioned, "But I like how you asked."

Come Not To Us

"What can I say liquor makes me loquacious. With a little luck there'll be a lady with me tonight."

"Loquacious?" frowned Peter.

"Com'on, I know just the song," hurried Doreen.

"I learned it in court three weeks ago," shouted Tony over his shoulder while Doreen led him by the hand into the living room. In a minute Peter heard the speakers of the stereo crack and pulse as Doreen set the needle on the record. The brass section exploded into house and soon Peter's friend and wife spun like tops careening around an ever bigger space among the party goers.

> They call you lady luck
> But there is room for doubt
> At times you have a very un-lady-like way
> Of running out...

The crowd pressed in from the other rooms to watch. Peter took the opportunity to circle around the now empty den through the side door of the kitchen. By greeting their friends and mingling Peter missed the passing hors d'oeurve tray a dozen times and the gin made his stomach scream for some reinforcements to soak up onslaught of alcohol. He sashayed from foot to foot with a deviled-egg in one hand and crudite in the other. He hummed softly along with the bars of *Luck Be A Lady* around a mouthful of finger food. He gave his best Sinatra spin returning to his drink when he saw Wendell leaning on the door jamb to peek furtively around the swinging door that separated the kitchen from the living room.

"Wendell!" belched Peter already losing volume control from this gin and tonic.

"Oh," started Wendell gently pushing the door back into place, "You scared the hell out of me." The dark shadow that fell over his face when he shut the door stuck under his eyes in sleepless black circles.

"What are you worried about? This is a party. Loosen up and get out there. Why are you standing in the corner checking around the door?"

"Don't you see what's going on out there?"

"Out where?"

"In your *own* living room for God's sake."

"They're dancing. So what?"

"You're just going to stand there while that abrasive attorney twirls your wife around the house?"

"Tony dances better than me and I'm hungry."

"I'm sure that isn't the only thing he does better than you."

Peter chuckled and walked over to Wendell. He put his inebriated arm around his cousin's shoulder and gave an uncharacteristic squeeze. Peter raised his eyebrows while he playfully puckered his lips together. He tilted his head left eye down, curled the tips of his fingers around the panel of the door and snuck a glance into the heart of the party. He saw Tony standing tall in the center of the room looking over Doreen's shoulder at a voluptuous red-head who slunk her way to the front of the amoebic circle of friends. She was one of Doreen's friends from college whose name Peter could never remember. The woman coquettishly ran her finger around the rim of her champagne flute while her shoulders undulated to the second and fourth beats of every measure. Peter whispered an aside to himself, "There's luck's lady tonight."

"What?" demanded Wendell.

"I said, do you think he's going to get lucky with my wife right in front of all our friends?"

"Peter, I'm sorry, but I've always thought this," Wendell paused not knowing if he should. "You're a damned idiot."

"Why thank you, Wendell. I'm so glad you could make it. Would you care for refreshment?" asked Peter holding out an empty tray.

"Well, I for one am not about to stand around. She's showing such blatant disregard for you right in front of your face and everyone you know. It boggles my mind how you can never see it. Can't you see the handwriting on the wall?"

"No, I'm too busy watching you bounce off them."

"Wake up man! I'd hate to know how she treats you alone at home. It's probably nothing a good slap wouldn't cure."

"Don't worry I'll never tell you," leveled Peter soberly.

The song ended and Wendell held the door open a crack with his foot. Doreen draped over Tony's arm in the finale of a dip like a black silk scarf. The room erupted in applause that segued into *I've Got You Under My Skin*. The crowd filled in and the bubbles of sound rose higher in the glass of the tittering red-head. Tony already assumed the debonair stance of her personal sommelier for the evening.

"Why are you here if you're just going to skulk around the kitchen complaining about who my wife dances with?"

"The hell if I know. You two invited me."

Peter ran down the guest list in his mind and couldn't remember putting Wendell anywhere on it. He did not recall seeing him arrive, yet here he stood brooding.

"Wendell, I'm sorry, but I've always thought this," Peter paused more for effect than reflection, "I never liked you."

Wendell rolled his bent fingers up and down like a wave of pistons. He glared at his cousin for a moment flaring his nostrils before he picked out the black knob of the back door. He cut a crow's line to it through Peter's shoulder. He rattled the cubes in Peter's bowl before the metal shade slapped against the window. The shade scratched back and forth to a stop and hung with all the annoyance of a disonant accordion.

Come Not To Us

"Jackass didn't grab his coat," said Peter.

Quickly the muffled music drew him out of the kitchen. He hoisted two silver trays over his shoulders and backed slowly through the door. He hummed a flat bar and folded back into the full sound of revelry.

> *Don't you know you fool, you never can win*
> *Use your mentality, wake up to reality*
> *But each time I do, just the thought of you*
> *Makes me stop before I begin*
> *cause I've got you under my skin.*

***

"Vatch vhere you valk," warned Otto. "Poison ivy ist all about. Da sind zhe small plants mit zhe outside leaves dhat look like zhey have spreading thumbs."

"Itching?"

"Scratching, like a Hund mit fleas."

"What are we seeing?"

"Das guest Haus."

"Any famous dignitaries?"

"Nein, but zum refreshing vomen friends."

The two men wound slowly around a stone lined path that led out the front door of the house. Ahead a pondside artesian well sprouted a simple A-frame roof atop two posts made of young trunks. It stood complete with a wooden lathe bucket hoisted up a brown rusted pulley. The bucket's steel handle hung on a short length of rope permanently tethered to an iron ring half way up one of the posts under the roof. The bottom of the pail rotted out a decade before and the rope length was three feet too short for the vessel to reach any of the water that lay underneath a metal hatch swung shut over the well's opening with a hinge and two handles.

"Why the well?" asked Peter as Otto led him to the left down a separate path away from the well. "The pond is just ten more feet. Couldn't you have just drawn water from there?"

"Stimmt."

"Meaning?"

"Certainly, but a bunker disguised as a vell ist not zu be found."

"So why tell me now? Keep the secret."

"Who can climb in it anymore? I am ninety-sechs jahre alt. I no longer look for places zu live."

"You didn't strike me as a bomb shelter kind of guy."

"It kept me busy near zhe guest Haus when visitors drove here from Chicago."

"You didn't invite me to stay," smiled Peter.

"Nein, I did not vant you in bed."

Brett Ramseyer

They walked past five foot thick willow trunks to a narrow deck surrounded by a dense row of cedars that rose up around the shallows of the pond where ancient trout fanned the gravel bottom with their tails. The thickness of the trees locked out the morning sun creating an aura of perpetual dusk.

The little brown house set into the tiny slope, a native of the forest. Moss grew under the eaves like the north side of a tree and the organic musk of rotting leaves mixed with the clean bite of the fronds of cedar foliage. The scents enveloped the architecture of the one story building. The simplicity of the less than two-hundred square feet honed Peter's approaching eye down to the striking leaded glass window that adorned the top half of the entry door. At the base of the window light collected in the heart of a blood red diamond that anchored the base of a three-dimensional illusion. It appeared as if a sky-scraper's corner jut out at Peter as stories stacked on top of each other in clear glass with small black rhomboid panes dividing them. The longer he stared at them the more the window mesmerized his senses. His eyes wavered out of focus and the sharp out pointing corner seemed to now swing in like French doors into a millionaire's brothel.

Otto fumbled a skeleton key in the lock before grunting the latch open. "Velcome zu my Taliesin."

Peter stooped first into the infinitesimal closeness of the entry way. He side-stepped left into a miniature sitting room. Two dark walnut benches built into opposite walls and nearly met in the center of the tiny room. A single brown shaded lamp stood on a spindly end table across from the door.

"What's the meaning of Taliesin?"

"Shining brow."

"I don't see the connection. This place doesn't look too sparkling. What other German names do you have for it?"

"Es ist nicht Deutsch. Es ist Welsh. Zhe Name comes from vun of your neighbors."

Peter's skin began to creep feeling Otto's eyes peer into the streets of his home. An uneasiness grew in his chest like the heavy weight of the death of a loved one pulling down on the heart before actually hearing the sad news.

"My neighbor?"

"Ja, Frank Lloyd Wright, zhe architect."

Peter's imperceptible smirk eased the tension in his heart. "His work is my neighbor, but not him."

"Of course, he's long dead, but not his ideas. The pane of glass in zhe door ist of his design und zhe Name I give mein Haus hier ist from his bastion of lust in Wisconsin."

Come Not To Us

"Taliesin?" Peter mulled it slowly in a whisper of recollection. "Taliesin. Taliesin."

"How can you not know zhe shtories of your own backyard?"

"You said he was long dead. How am I supposed to know?"

"Geschicte, Herr Sonderling, Geshichte. I told you. No one knows the true history. Don't you valk past zhe large homes he built in your neighborhood?"

"I have."

"Vell look at zhem. You'll zee his life in his art. His low horizontal buildings, zhat hug zhe earth, such unassuming zimplicity. He used zhem only to sneak up on zhe werld und his clients. He vas a married man mit a Haus brimming mit children, zhen he met Mrs. Cheney."

"Cheney."

"Ja, Mamah Borthwick Cheney, a middle class voman married zu a vealthy engineer. It shtarted zimply like zhe low slung house Wright vas designing for her husband; it vas only a ride in Herr Wright's car. I imagine she liked zhe flow of zhe wind srough her hair. Soon enough zhey sailed avay zu Europe."

"He threw away his life," said Peter quietly looking down at his hands.

"He shtarted a new vun. Vhen zhey returned zu America he vas changed. He called his architecture 'organic' and moved his new mistress into a rolling hill in Wisconsin. He built 'Taliesin' zu eshcape into zhe earth. It vas his hiding place from zhe shtale Idee of American morality."

"So, this is Taliesin," said Peter holding his arms up around him and nearly touching both sides of the room.

"Only in Name und shpirit. I built und designed it myself on zhe foundation of an old garage." Otto leaned into a short hall that passed a closet sized lavatory overlooking the pond. Peter followed him slowly pushing cobwebs down ahead of his face as they cracked through latch of the bedroom door. Otto entered and walked around the foot of the bed and stood before a bank of windows across the wall. He turned around and looked down at the once white blanket pocked with the pellets of squirrel scat. He lifted his cane and swiped it across the bed and some black grains pattered to the floor like the sound of bouncing rice. His right eye leaked a little and he chuckled.

"Zhe afternoons I've shpent in zhis Bett," he started.

Peter rubbed his hands together to knock off the feeling of filth that covered them. "You and Frank Lloyd Wright," joked Peter uncomfortably.

The joke fell flat like a heavy book on an oak table and silence filled the room. Then as suddenly as it all began Otto jerked awake as from a trance and began leading Peter out of the guest house. 'Nein," he said as he scuffed along. "Dozens of vomen, but ve must be heading back. I, like Wright, built my Taliesin mit only vun door."

"So?"

"Zo his sins talleyed up faster zhan vun of his Barbados servants would have liked. Zhe black man shnapped on a calm afternoon. He lit zhe Haus on fire vhile Wright, Mrs. Cheney und ozhers lunched. Zhe party ran srough zhe only door vhere zhe dishtraught servant waited zu murder zhem mit a hatchet. He hacked seben of zhem zu pieces."

"Oh my God! I didn't know that was how Frank Lloyd Wright died."

"He didn't, but Mrs. Cheney and two of her children vere killed. Wright vatched zhem bleed zu death. He zaw zhem inhale zhere last breaths next to his blazing building."

"That's terrible," said Peter as he watched Otto turn the key in the lock. "Was the servant insane?"

"Ach," Otto sighed, "It's just alvays been hard zu find gut help."

Peter could not keep himself from laughing. He stayed behind Otto within the boundaries of the path not minding the slothful pace they took back to the house. Thinking, Peter looked down at Otto's heels in front of him. He started counting the steps by bobbing his head.

"You did with visitors there while your wife was just two hundred feet up the path in the house?"

"Ja," said Otto not turning back to look.

"Weren't you afraid of being caught?"

"Never!"

"Never? I find that hard to believe."

"I alvays had a varning."

The two men walked up three stone steps into the small lawn clearing in front of the house. Otto pointed up high almost to the roof of the house. Another small piece jut out casting a dark shadow on the siding. As they walked closer Peter could see a black bell suspended high above them. Hanging down from it twisted a calcified white rope. Its frayed end stopped five feet from the periwinkle that choked in around the base of the house.

"Mein varning bell," said Otto. "If lunch vere ready or I had been gone zu lang, Anna vould redeem me mit tree tugs." At that Otto gave three healthy pulls that sent a salvo of peels resonating through the valley. A pair of resting crows vaulted from their perch and scattered into the forest.

"And then what?"

"Und zhen I vould walk home."

"Just like that."

"Ja. Don't be zo surprised. Da ist no such ding as a gut husband, only vives who undershtand zhem. "

"She let you back in the house."

Come Not To Us

"Naturlich," said Otto calmly moving toward his front steps, "Zhe only souvenir she brought me from her holiday in Egypt vas syphilis."

Brett Ramseyer

19

Peter sidestepped his way out of the car and nearly tripped over inner tubes and partially inflated rafts. He arrested his fall with a hand on the wall where he knocked a heavy pair of oars off the wall still connected to their rusty oarlocks. They slipped with audible friction over a lounge chair and clattered to the concrete in unison with his curse that he sheepishly clipped short at the sight of Michael's bare feet.

His son's dripping shorts clung to his small body and quickly splattered a circle around him on the floor. His wet hourglass tracks curved around the entrance evaporating faster than Peter's anger.

"Daddy, you're home."

"Yup, just now Michael"

"Guess what I've got to show you."

"Slow down," said Peter high stepping behind the powerful pull of a six-year-olds imagination. "I'm tripping over these oars and mattresses."

"All right Dad, you found them!" yipped Michael releasing this father's wrist and snatching up the oars. He dragged them around the corner shouting, "Come on! I wanna show you."

With less than breathless excitement Peter walked along two furrows in the dirt of the path. They meandered past the cottage to flow into two light streaks of bent grass through the lawn to disappear over the break wall. As he neared the water's edge he expected to see a boat ready to shove off into the lake with Michael at the helm. Instead his oars stood buried in the narrow strip of beach while the boy wound white nylon rope around them. He had anchored a half circle string of rafts from one oar to the other. Peter stood three feet above the sand and looked down to see his daughter looking straight up over her head with her mouth wide open and her cheeks smeared with silt. She wore only her diaper that strained against the weight of the water trapped in it. She waddled back and forth between the two oars with her bulging duck bottom waggling behind her. She gave out little squeals as she stomped her feet into the ooze that sent splashes all around. All the while she said, "Daddy, I's wimming. I's wimming."

The rafts at the apex of their arc only ventured ten feet into the water where Michael stood now facing the shore up to his knees. He bent over cupping the water in his hands and splashing it back toward Claudie. "See Dad? I made a swim circle out of my own magination."

"I see."

"I gotta keep Claudie from drownding."

Brett Ramseyer

"He's a good boy," said Grandma Claudia from the dock. She sat calmly in a deck chair sipping a lemonade while watching over the children. Specks of sunlight that passed through the wide brim of her white straw hat gave her a more cheerful appearance than Peter was accustomed to seeing in her countenance. "He's a good boy who knows how to look out for his family."

***

"How did you get here?" stammered Peter at the sight of his mother leafing through the piles of documents at the table of the cottage kitchen.

"Michael's a good boy. He drove me up. I decided that it was time that I start looking out for my family."

Peter's face burned red at the idea of his inadequacy. His innards collapsed to his scrotum to wallow guiltily in the seat of his transgression. She knew. It was as if she filtered down in the flecks of dust that glowed in last evening's pink light. She fell quietly, slowly, painfully like a stout hand toward a shoulder to twist him around to look up at his actions. She landed tonight, four fingers on a collar bone pulling and cracking his brittle resistance.

"It's more than a five hour drive."

"Six. We stopped to eat twice. Michael's growing.

"Where is he?"

"On the dock, he said he would catch dinner. – You look hungry son."

"Not as much as you might think."

Claudia stood up and crossed over to the stove. She pulled an old mug from the cupboard stained permanently brown. Scalded coffee flowed in a torrent over the lip of pot she'd unearthed from the pantry. Drops clung to the side and left a crescent drying on the white enamel of the stove top. She passed the drink to her son.

"I couldn't find a coffee or a teapot."

"I don't usually try to stay awake when I'm here. Coffee seems unnecessary."

"Mrs. Van Duinnen showed us where you hang the spare key."

Peter felt an itch he dare not scratch, but "How's Rita this morning?"

"Worried, like a good mother. Like your mother."

"Why?"

"Maybe it's because you aren't sleeping around here as much as you used to."

Peter pursed his lips and nodded slowly. A screaming silence rose between them. Peter pinched his bottom lip between thumb and index finger. He looked blankly at his mug smiled a liars empty grin and said, "A lot of work to do around here. You're sitting in the research library and the construction site is through the living room."

"It's quite a lot," she said. She picked up the falsehood like cash. She tucked it down the front of her shirt like a secret payment of debt. She hid it from mention. She hid it from view near her heart. She leaned back in her chair to assure herself that Michael still stood at the end of the dock casting into the lake and Mrs. Van Duinnen did not pop over with a plate of sandwiches. This retribution a mother only allows a son when she has wronged him by tucking so many filthy bills in his pockets since his birth.

The staggering expense of her loan could not be paid off in decades of Peter's deceit. She clutched the neck of her blouse closed like the iron bars of a teller's window in the midst of a panic. Claudia had invested so heavily in deception that she cornered the market, but Peter now tried to buy the truth with lies. She stood now fearfully peering through the gates at her own flesh peddling the only currency he knew. She balanced the facts written in the ledger of her memory against the run about to be made on the vault of her heart.

Bankrupt she sat in the chair like an empty sack.

Claudia looked around her at the documents obscuring the table. It amazed her to see paper in so many shades, not colors, but shades of white. The ecru receipts of a life with Isaac assured her as gently as her husband's laughter. She fanned the papers out with her hand and imagined his warm pulse against her skin. Her courage began to rise enough to stir through the creamy stock listings in which Isaac so carefully grew their life savings. She began to see their wealth, not money, but the wealth of a life built together that rose from such frigid ashes.

Emboldened she looked to the blond newspaper clippings that spiraled up at the edges like flames. So many times she attempted to burn these images from her memory. She imagined them curling into black cinders that broke apart at the slightest touch and rode away forever on a breath of wind, but today she looked at them. She saw the doctors timing their torture and touting their discoveries. She saw a frozen and trembling forearm lolling in their hands. She envisioned Peter's father. She envisioned her husband. She felt her strength rising and they no longer blurred in her mind. They rose together into the clear combination that might open where she safely packed away her demon truths so long ago.

She started again. "It's quite a lot that Isaac collected over the years."

"Why did he keep it all, Mom?"

"To give me courage I think."

"Courage for what?"

"To start again –"

"It's been hard for both of us without Dad. It's not really starting over, but continuing on."

"I don't mean now, Peter."

"If not now, when?"

"Forty years ago."

"You need courage now for forty years ago?" Peter walked his frustration to the sink where he jettisoned his untasted coffee down the drain. "These conversations never lead anywhere with you, Mother. You drove for six hours at a time when I don't need you looking over my shoulder with Michael in tow. What I need is some solitude because these cryptic stories never end."

"No Peter," she pleaded, "They've never begun."

"Stop riddling!" screamed Peter slamming his mug on the counter. He shattered the ceramic into pieces that left the handle intact like an ear in his hands. "It's bad enough that I bed some trailer whore last night without coming home to find you sitting at the table waiting like I'm late coming home from the prom. Between you and Rita clambering around for a life, you've managed to destroy mine." Peter's firing eyes shot their anger and he said, "I don't want you here," barely above a whisper.

Claudia locked onto her son's gaze without fear. She walked slowly toward him and clasped her hands around his. "As I said before, I'm here to start looking out for my family."

"There's not much left to save. I sweated away the last of my dignity in a barn."

"It doesn't matter."

"Oh shit, not you too."

"Me too?"

"Because God is dead, or doesn't care, or just watches us for entertainment in some sick movie, right?"

"No Peter, because I'm not Dornröschen." Claudia slipped the mug handle from Peter's hands and began to cradle it across her chest in her folded arms.

"Dad told the fairytales, remember?"

"You're so terribly wrong, Peter. I did. I told the fairytales and he gave you your family history. I don't know how many times he winced at the barbs of my tongue when I would catch him telling you bedtime stories that horrified me, but he insisted that you loved them."

With incredulous sarcasm Peter said, "So am I the descendent of sorcerers of dwarves? Wait, I've always been a little short- "

"Isaac was Dornröschen; it's how we met."

"In a field of thorns?"

"The death camps were nothing but thorns, Peter. We couldn't move anywhere without being bloodied. Can't you understand? It's why

Come Not To Us

I've withheld the truth for so long. I couldn't face the memories. I had to put them aside because the two faces I loved were so tangled in that bleeding past that you and Isaac were all I could bare to remember."

"So start remembering," demanded Peter like a prosecutor at trial.

***

"Kummer!" shouted Hauptsturmführere Rascher. "Is trial seven ready."

"Ja, Doktor," blew in with a trace of snow through an open steel door. Dark haired Doktor Peter Kummer backed into the laboratory with his gloved hands under the armpits of trial number seven. He waddled backwards and swung a naked and unconscious prisoner onto a cold table draped with a white sheet.

"Shut the Gott damn door!" scolded Rascher. "It's freezing out there you dummkopf."

"Jawohl, Herr Doktor," chirped the guard who dropped the trials ankles to the table before quickly clicking his own heels together and raising a stiff salute. He moved quickly through the opening slamming the door behind him.

Rascher walked over to the prostrate man. He picked up a clipboard on his way and began to scan the data. "Kummer, how was the specimen prepared."

Kummer sauntered over leafing through his own black leather bound notes reading, "19:00 thrown into the River Wuerm - 19:15 stripped naked – 19:30 set in courtyard – 01:00 specimen still running in place – 03:00 stumbling – "

"A fighter, this one."

"- 05:00 specimen collapsed."

"They all succumb sooner or later," said Rascher sucking in a monstrous breath. He removed his SS gloves and prodded the man's abdomen with his bare fingertips. "Ah, Ich liebe Dachau im winterzeit! December's winds always blow the flesh a beautiful blue."

"Ja," said Kummer, "As a child I had cat's eye marbles the same color."

"Na ja, look at his scrotum. His marbles are in his throat." Rascher gurgled through an unaccompanied chuckle. "What is his temperature?"

"Sechs-und-zwanzig Punkt seben Grade."

"He has a chance."

"Veilliecht, shall we use the sun lamps or hot bath?

"Neither."

"Irrigation? Herr Doktor we know he'll die," argued Kummer. "You know Himmler will increase pressure to show results in our work. The Russian front will-"

"Bitte sei ruhig, Kummer. My wife Karoline und I just last night supped with the intrepid Reichsführer Himmler und we discussed a new strategy in warming."

"He's not a Doktor nor a scientist. Should we really be using his advice in such an important experiment for the Reich?"

"Stimmt, und even you will find it more entertaining than a bath. Where is your rat assistant?"

"Claudia?"

"You use her name?"

"Naturlich, what do you suggest?"

"A German assistant not a Jew."

"She's too knowledgeable to discharge."

"Luckily so are you or I could have the Gestapo open your files for consorting with the filth of the fatherland."

"I don't know what you are talking about."

"Bring her in."

"I don't think she should-"

"Bring her in!" roared Rascher, "Or do you find the trial's night time accommodations delightful enough to check into them for the evening?"

"Ein Moment, Herr Doktor," replied Kummer weakly. He turned around smartly and exited through an interior door. He stopped in the hall and placed his hands on his knees. Not knowing Rascher's plan he wanted to run to Claudia, wrap his trench coat around her and smuggle her through the gates of the camp. He could not make himself move. He buried his face in his hands and slowly ran his fingers through his black hair.

Behind him he heard the steel feet of the table groan across the frigid floor as Rascher dragged it into position. Kummer started down the hall to the lab. His quivering fist struggled to find the keyhole. Inside Claudia kept herself busy cleaning the same test tubes for the third time of the day. She heard the door open, but kept her head down and face to her work.

"Claudia, komm," was all he said.

Doktor Peter Kummer used her name in the afternoons. After a morning of experiments his blood would run thick, like polluted oil of an over worked machine. He would call her to his office where they could be alone. He would lock the door and treat this Jew differently than all the rest.

He spotted her the day she entered the camp. Her face struck him during the inspection in roll call square. She stared blankly in the line until he stood in front of her. The other women stood embarrassed by their nakedness trying to cover their breasts and genitals, but she stood unapologetically with her hands at her sides. He pressed his fingertips up beneath her chin feeling her glands. Her blankness turned to ferocity the instant he touched her skin. She widened her stance and stood straight to bolster her up. Her pupils shrank and seared an indelible mark in his consciousness. She held her focus until she made him look away. Kummer pinked with embarrassment, but recovered himself quickly enough to feel the firmness of her breast with his upturned hand. He waved her into a small group of select prisoners and continued with his inspections.

The culling of the new arrivals usually did not take long. The weak, the infirm, the violent and the genuinely ugly marched to the right. If not sent to Linz for extermination they marched to the shooting range outside the main camp for target practice. The rest worked unmercifully for a few days, but not fed and soon enough added to the cloud cover that would waft over Munich. To the left the guards floured the able bodied with delousing powder, shaved their heads, and issued baggy pants and a shirt. The guards would lead them to one of the long line of thirty-two barracks to climb onto a wooden rack that would torment their nights with frozen splinters, but a minute percentage stood near the medical tables in the center of the square until the doctors led them away.

No Jews officially worked in the hospital. It was verboten. Yet, Claudia folded linens, counted syringes and washed test tubes. No Jews officially worked in the hospital, but all the death candidates sleeping in the barracks knew the faces of the few. They still wore cheeks with too much color and ribs with too much meat. A buffer of space and stares usually followed the select around the camp.

Claudia lived in her senses, but took no joy in them. She lived a lifetime each time Doktor Kummer summoned her to his office. He did not force her in nor coax, he asked. In the beginning he only handed her treats. A half eaten dark chocolate bar sent her stale mouth awash in a syrup she could barely swallow until he pushed a glass of milk across his desk at her. She left soon after and shivered through the night in her bunk assured that her entire barrack would catch the scent of her breath and tear her jaw from her skull to pick the black sweetness from her teeth like scavengers pulling gold fillings from the dead.

When she awoke in the morning to the echoing "Rrrauss! Stehen Sie Auf!" her amazement drove her quickly to her job. Soon each day she fell into the terrible habit of wondering when he would call to her. She awaited the senses of tinned meat, buttered bread, and the wonderful – Kase. She could smell the cold musk of the cheese on the desk and she stood once again with her hands at her sides, but today he wanted more. For the first time, he too stood and spoke. He only passed the food across his desk in the past. He would sit back in his chair and slide it toward her. He would watch her eat and she would leave. This day the cheese sat unmoved and he stood. "I must collect on your bill," and he touched her breast with his upturned hand. Claudia, a nineteen-year-old girl no longer believed in twenty. She believed in the musk of the cheese and of the Doktor's touch. She stared with a similar intensity as in the square, but her gaze was not at him.

When he finished she winced at the sharp bite of her treat. Her teeth carved slowly to focus her senses anew. Her pain was not loving and her taste was not joy, yet she ate without remorse.

***

"It has eaten at me through the decades, Peter. In some ways I don't know how it hasn't come pouring out of the holes in me."

"Yet the only drops I've tasted mother have been those Dad has saved for me."

"He never kissed me awake."

"You said the fairytales were real and you already contradict yourself."

"It was I who kissed him. I kissed him awake. I brought him to life." A tear trembled on her lashes. She looked away and wanted to stop.

"Tell me the story." Peter commanded soberly.

"In the camp hospital they froze prisoners." She lifted up the yellowed clipping with Rascher holding a limp wrist. "Sometimes with water," she pointed, "but Isaac they threw out into winter. They plunged him in the river filled with the muck of the dead and left him stripped in the wind for an entire night. Two doctors led me into the room where they brought him. Someone had ordered them to thaw their experiments with women. They watched me undress and told me to climb on top of the table. I straddled Isaac and they ordered me to copulate with him until they were satisfied. I wept on him, but they ordered me on. I shook with the pain of the frozen man between my legs and hot lash at my back when I stopped. I vomited on the floor and one doctor left. Doctor Rascher stayed on to order more and more depravity."

Her monotonous, blank rhythm stopped and Peter picked up the clipping. "Rascher?" he said quietly. Peter began to slowly circle the table holding the clipping stepping on his ordered piles.

"He ordered me to kiss him. He ordered me to kiss him," she sobbed snapping the mug handle in her hands as she groaned.

Peter took her feeble shoulders in his hands and said, "I have to know."

Claudia choked on her own throat, coughed and said in a whisper, "He awoke. My kiss on his chilly face-"

"You're the princess!" blurted from Peter's childhood and he suddenly felt very small. He was shrinking into himself. The walls expanded away from him and he shot backwards through a tunnel at the speed of light.

20

Peter awoke in pool of his own sweat. His infant brow burned hot to his mother's touch. She cradled him close to her chest praying that his fever would pass. Her days in Augsburg brought nothing, but hunger pangs and isolation. She delivered her new son in a shelter for the displaced. Gray faced soldiers missing their limbs watched disinterestedly as she endured a sick child through his birth. A confused old woman attended her with little knowledge of midwifery, but enough of calves to help the newborn stay alive.

The colicky baby cried incessantly and soon turned the soldier's eyes from indifference to disdain. A Jew and her pitiful whelp caterwauling throughout the night were not the ointment for their itching stumps nor defeated ideology. Claudia watched their ire grow proportionally to their volume of discussion amongst themselves. She left before morning into the summer streets of Augsburg.

By morning her exhausted arms clutched her son, but wished to wave a hello in a search for Americans. She remembered their stunned faces in April, 1945, as their tanks and Jeeps rumbled into the gates of camp. The prisoners milled in bewilderment when the SS left Dachau. The guards were clearly edgy for weeks and in the last days their brutality reached a fever pitch. Thousands of death candidates loaded trains or marched double time into the night, but not Claudia. Doktor Kummer stowed her in the bowels of the central kitchen where she and her ample womb would find the necessary nourishment. He checked her three times a day until the middle of April when he brought her a store of goods.

"Will this be enough for a time?" Kummer asked.

Claudia sensed the uneasiness in his voice. "Are the Allies advancing?"

"Nonsense, Liebchen," deflected Kummer, "The Wehrmacht is only days from victory. The Americans do not have the constitution for war and soon will lose their foothold on the continent."

"That's good for you."

"And you. In a few weeks I'll move you out into the country. I'll establish you in a Bavarian Bauernhof to raise good German milk cows."

"No medicine in your future Herr Doktor?"

"Even cattle catch cold."

"Like the men you've frozen?"

"No," he looked at her from the corner of his eyes, "But even a good farmer must castrate some cows for the good of the herd. I like to think that

I've improved your stock. No matter, I may only be free to visit late tomorrow night. Inspection coming, I hate to be caught with documents in disarray."

"Bis später – 'til later," said Claudia looking down. He locked the door behind him with the cha-clunk of a thick metal bolt and never returned.

When the door opened again those American faces looked in at another atrocity. Those men exchanged more glances with each other and spoke quietly. Their rifles hung on their backs with cold barrels. Their well rested, energetic eyes convinced Claudia to hold their strong hands and they gently pulled Claudia to her feet. She looked for those same eyes and helping hands in Augsburg, but the gentle energy of April already swayed toward exasperation in August. There were too many hungry, too many homeless, too many cracked lips gasping for assistance that these seeming men of the spring transformed into boys by fall. Their answers to the state of the world failed millions, so helping one Jewish woman and her newborn child confused them even further.

For the Nazis it was simple. Concentrate the Jews in one place. Funnel them into one factory of death or another. House them just long enough to keep the pile of ashes used for fertilizer from snuffing out the flame of the furnaces. Spread them in the fields, flush them down the rivers or cast them to the winds.

The Americans struggled just the same. What to do with the Jews? And in the most sincere of ironies they landed at the same conclusion by different means. At Dachau Claudia forgot the outside world. She plodded for years, marching in place between the coils of electrified wire. When the Americans liberated the camp her skepticism squelched any sense of elation. By August her reservations proved true in her mind. The outside world forgot about her. Now instead of Dachau's confinement she wandered in step to an American tune of freedom syncopated with the blues of chaos. With the Nazis she knew her place, unimaginable misery to soon precede agonizing death. With the Americans her place stood somewhere else, no matter where she stood. In the end she sensed the same feelings from her American 'friends' that she felt inside the walls of the camp. They wanted her and countless others to evaporate into the air, to float away on some barge, or to crawl under the earth. Their answer, a Diaspora, like the ashes only she felt certain they did not expect better crops.

So, she moved twice a week with her son Peter on her hip. From one camp, staging area, city, depot, port to another she marched. She begged food, took any offering, turned to another when denied. Her lonely quest took her to the north. She asked anyone who would listen if they knew her, her family or anyone she ever met. She lusted after any connection no matter how small on which to take hold. She needed one tendril, one root on which to feed her hunger for place.

Come Not To Us

In the week of the New Year she traveled to Hamburg. The piles of rubble dominated all and stood silent like eerie moguls under a fresh blanket of snow. Near the wasted docks of the river she warmed her hands over a barrel one by one. She kept her baby in plain view even in the cold because it offered her the only ticket to a barrel-side stance.

The orange flames gave her a jaundiced glow in the evening and she waited quietly until she reached sufficient warmth to begin asking her circle of friends for a place to hide from the winter winds. Suddenly a gust of him blew in front of her, his arms outspread before they clamped down on her back making Peter cry.

"I found you! I found you! I found you!" he blurted incoherently through his tears as some alarmed men tried to pry him off. When they separated Claudia looked at him confused. His gaunt face much older than hers frightened her, not because of unfamiliarity, but because she remembered.

"Leave him be!" she shouted. "We met in the camps!"

The two broke the circle hand in hand and she did not question to where he led her. For the first time in her memory she did not feel alone. He simply repeated, "My princess," again and again.

She knew not how this "Isaac" booked passage for the three of them aboard a ship or where they might land once the voyage ended, but she followed. Much like the Final Solution these three ashes of the Holocaust floated down the Elbe and out to sea fleeing from themselves for eternity.

***

"Is that why you kissed Dad at his funeral?" said Peter holding a box of tissue in front of him by the tips of his fingers.

"It had worked before," snuffled Claudia defiantly waving the box aside. "No tissues, Peter, let them run. It's creeks and rivers for me. I've pent up the tributaries to my pain for forty years."

"I think we came to the right place for the dam to break."

"Pentwater?"

"Sounds perfect."

"But what's down stream?"

"How can we ever know that?"

"We look at our children," said Claudia soberly. "I've never looked too far down stream at you. I've been so busy clinging to my island of illusion."

"Oh, mom you –"

"I set you adrift without so much as an oar of knowledge to row your way home again. I think I was afraid if you saw the ugliness inside of your life you'd be apt to row away."

"And here I am living like a sailor in port with the nearest barmaid. I found the hideous parts of me without your help."

Brett Ramseyer

"We are a sorry pair, Peter," said Claudia reaching out to cover her son's hands.

"More so in regret."

"And pity."

They slumped in a bereft silence. Claudia's bony fingertips read hard work in Peter's battered hands. The cool smooth pressure of her disappearing prints could not help themselves, but to circle over the day old scabs on his knuckles. His coarse and chapped hands bore the immolation of his days of construction.

"I miss Dad."

"You've no idea," admitted Claudia.

"You too?"

"I miss that you didn't know your father."

Peter raised his eyebrow in confused question. "What? So you tell me that you saved Dad's life in the death camps. That doesn't change the fact that Dad was one of the kindest most generous men I knew. How many times did he hug me, help me, sing my praises, for God's sake he damn near mothered me. You, you were so distant and cold. It's like you pulled the winter off his body and stored it in your heart."

"The day I met Isaac, your father was in the room, but he wasn't freezing below me on the table."

Incredulity grew across Peter's face like an ice crystal. It spread jagged and irregular, cutting into him with all the unique and unwanted individuality of a snowflake in May. His lips drew straight and hard across his slippery teeth before they cracked with the slow careful annunciation of epiphany.

"HOW OLD AM I?"

"Do you have the Gerburtsschein?"

Peter pulled his wallet from his back pocket and opened the tri-fold. The fragile paper crackled lightly after he wet his index finger to separate edges of the sheet that pressed together. As it fell open he lay his hands upon it and drew them away from each other smoothing it out on the table. Claudia took it carefully in two fingers. The wrinkles on her wizened forehead seemed to melt and Peter saw an expression on his mother's face he never saw before. Her eyes opened ever wider. She held the paper six inches from the end of her nose focused some five thousand miles away. She hung in a purgatory trance between nostalgia and regret that made Peter sit quietly and wait for a reply.

"It's all here," she said, "Your truth that Isaac held in trust. I decided we should burn this long ago. When I could not find it he told me he had done it for me. He said, 'It isn't a mother's place to destroy her child's past.' He made me feel safe when he said it. His chivalry to save me from an unpleasant sight calmed me. His protection felt warm. It was such a ridiculous gesture as if I hadn't seen the evils of the world. The story of burning this paper was probably the only lie that man ever told that I didn't ask him to tell. Even this is the first page of fiction I dictated about your life."

"What is the truth then?" Peter pleaded.

Claudia drew a breath and reported, "Unbekannt. It is what I told the officials in Augsburg when they asked who your father was. The clerk wrote it down without question. He didn't look up. His ashen face never peered up from under his mop of gray hair. He stamped your birth quickly into existence and passed the certificate and me along as quickly as he could. He made it easy to be false because he didn't care."

"I was born in 1945? I'm nearly forty." The shock of it all barely registered inside his hollow chest

Claudia reached across the table and grasped a yellow clipping. "In a way I've always expected to be caught. I named you for confession." She held the clipping of a historical discovery up to her son. "Doktor *Peter* Kummer was your father."

Peter looked at his eerie reflection from more than thirty years before. This doctor stared back with the cold look of calculation. His dark eyes shone with the dull sheen of flat ink covering an accounting page. He seemed a systemization of tables, figures and raw data. His two thick eyebrows marked his face like two straight negative signs that multiplied into the positive resemblance that Peter K. Sonderling washed in the mirror every morning. He stood from his chair and walked into the living room to stand in the threshold of the entrance to the sun room under construction. He looked out over the lawn to watch Michael heave his line far out into the rippling lake with a dexterity of the wrist Peter felt he did not possess.

"He was in the room," continued Claudia, "When I met Isaac. He came to find me that day to bring me into that room."

"That man," said Peter pointing "Was not my father. My father built this room with me. My father raised me in the suburbs of Chicago and died last winter."

"Stop Peter!" begged Claudia.

"My father, Isaac Sonderling was the bedrock on which our family stood!"

"Isaac was as sterile as a stone!" erupted from her mouth and Peter froze. "Your father stole Isaac's children from him. Herr Doktor Kummer guarded me in the camps like his pet mouse and when his superior ordered me into the room to revive Isaac your father acquiesced like a frightened child. He stood sentinel when he knew his child was in my belly. He allowed Doktor Rascher to order me into an act like some sexually deviant puppet. You are a child of weakness Peter, mine and your father's. My weakness has turned to lies and your father's weakness turned into cruelty."

Brett Ramseyer

"You're telling me my father was a murdering Nazi. Of course he was cruel."

"He was ashamed of putting me through such pain. His jealousy of those around me grew so furiously that I still wake nights shuddering from what he did. He was a scientist at heart. In his own mind he followed the protocols of science in search of answers. He forgot that we were people too. To him we Jews were only subjects to be prodded and studied. He ran his tests on cold and altitude to discover the outer reaches of human existence. Instead he discovered a far more terrible secret. He found that the depths of evil inside him had no bounds."

"The Nazi Doktors always ran dangerous experiments on the prisoners. I watched them put men in compression chambers to test the effects of high altitude flight on the human being. I saw men whose eardrums exploded. Their inner ear oozed down the sides of their heads until they dashed their skulls against a brick wall in an effort to kill themselves. I've seen Doktors shoot healthy men in the leg in order to leisurely daub experimental concoctions on their wounds to see if they could quell the bleeding. These and many more terrible experiments were done in the name of a science that had no purpose other than to torture us, but even in these Doktor Kummer had a tiny element of mercy in him. When the experiment was finished he always killed the subject with a sudden injection to the heart."

"I saw their unbelievable cruelty working in the camp experimental hospital and I heard the primal screams that seeped through the walls every day. I always said a relieved prayer when a scream would suddenly cease and never begin again. I always knew that the injection had carried off another soul away from the hell we suffered."

"That is what I expected for the man I had revived from the cold. I knew he was not dead when I left the room, but he would be before the week was out. One of the only smiles I saw from a subject in the hospital was a man they successfully revived from hypothermia. Doktor Rascher congratulated the man on a successful recovery and patted his wrist. The man gave a weak grin before the Doktor turned back around from a table and plunged a needle deep into the man's chest. He died instantly with his eyes peeled wide open like boiled eggs. It was the chill of those eyes that shivered me more than plastic skin of Isaac underneath me. That is what I assumed would happen to him."

"What did happen?" asked Peter feeling the whirling pull of his ancestors. They turned him back and forth from Isaac to Kummer and around in a dizzying pattern that threatened to pull him into a vortex of confliction. He began to mindlessly pick up the tools lying around the unfinished sun room.

Come Not To Us

"The worst possible thing, Doktor Kummer didn't kill Isaac. His hate ran too deep to let him die quickly. Not long after the thawing experiment I took part in, Kummer told me of exciting genetic testing he pitched to Rascher as a possibility to do some of his own ground breaking work. Rascher of course was a darling of the Nazi party and would let no one outshine him in research. His request was denied. Kummer was once again emasculated by his superior so he emasculated Isaac."

Peter caught a glint amid the spiral shavings of wood that littered the floor. He brushed them carefully aside where he picked up a missing drill bit. He twisted the shaft between his index finger and thumb and watched the spinning curl bore harmlessly into the air. He sat down weeping in the dust that quickly absorbed the drops of his tears.

Brett Ramseyer

21

Air raced over Peter's paste covered tongue. The sudden spasm of his diaphragm simultaneously pulled the air in and Peter to an upright position. The air stopped abruptly in the back of his throat and vanished. His body hung in inert shock like an apoplectic confusion. He heard only half of the second ring of the bell before someone quickly snatched the handset from the cradle. The frenetic tone still hovered in the air like the echo of a lonely wolf.

He gave his head a tiny rattle and pressed the meat of his thumbs into his eye sockets until the pressure turned the morning's diffused light from red, to black and finally to white beneath his eyelids.

Intermittent mumbling replaced the bell's echo. Each muted burst of speech ended in a higher pitch than it began, until Michael rang out clearly. He leaned up the stairs pressing the mouth piece to his chest, "Daaaddd! – Hey DAD!"

Peter swung his legs over the side of the bed, "What?!"

"Phone."

"Who is it? I'm sleeping." Peter ducked through the hoop of a shirt and walked to the head of the stairs.

"I don't know. I can hardly understand him. He talks like he's got a half-pound of sauerkraut in his mouth."

"Otto?" said Peter only to himself.

"He said your name and sort of growled 'Oddo. Oddo.'"

Peter knit his brows in a struggle to understand why he might call. Michael looked at his father and held the handset in front of him with two fingers pressing together on the chord. The dread seemed to pass unspoken between father and son. Michael curled up his lip and looked at the phone like a bulging-eyed mouse that just had its neck snapped flat in a trap. Peter took it from him and Michael returned to a stool at the counter to rejoin his softening cereal.

"Hello?"

"Peter, komm."

"Otto?"

"Jetzt Peter, komm," gasped through the phone.

"My family is here I can't –"

"Das Ende ist hier. Komm schnell" begged the phone.

Claudia looked in from the living room quizzically. Her expression of pure inquiry made Peter's decision. "I'll be there in twenty minutes," was all Peter said. The cord slacked in front of him as he walked to the wall to hang up.

"Where will you be?" she asked.

"Helping a friend a little south."

"Now?" said Michael. "You promised me last night you'd help me put the boat in this morning."

"I know, but this is important."

"So's fishing. We have to drive home tomorrow."

"You're sixteen now. Why don't you ask Bill if you can borrow his truck.

"Really?"

"Yeah, if it's all right with him it is fine with me. Tell him you'll just drive across Longbridge to put in for an hour or so up stream and be back to the landing. I'll stop there on my way back and we'll go together.

"Great!" slurped Michael through his cereal. He lifted his bowl and threw back the bottom half of his breakfast. He grabbed a rod from the corner and sprang for the door. He turned quickly before he left and pulled his fishing hat down over his eyes. "Be sure to look for me down stream on your way back."

"I'll look for you down stream," assured Peter. He brushed past his mother up the stairwell. She leaned into him, but his attention did not pick up the cues. He needed to dress quickly.

When Peter returned he sat in a kitchen chair to pull on and lace his shoes. Claudia grabbed his arm with concern and he shrugged her off. "This is serious mother. Please step aside."

She turned her right palm up and grabbed his chin. "She isn't worth it Peter," she said gravely into his eyes.

"She?" he stopped, "Who?"

"The other woman."

"Mom, I'm alright," Peter exhaled in a short burst through his nose. The right side of his mouth almost rose, but it was not a guilty grin. He took his mother's hand down from his face and put it carefully between his two palms. "I'm doing something for Dad." Claudia rocked back on her heels and gave Peter room to stand. He looked down into her eyes. He scanned the swelling curve of her tears that clung to her eyes like a dome of water in an over brimming cup.

***

The white china cup lay on the floor in the middle of the opening between the kitchen and the dining nook. Peter zeroed on this first sign of trouble after he pushed his way through the un-answering pink door. He slapped it first with the grating sound of the brass knocker before his silent wait turned to bottom fisted pounding.

Come Not To Us

The cup rested on its side with the handle finally stopping its tumble. Inside a small puddle of coffee was already shrinking into a stain. Peter followed similar puddles around the corner of the wall to a small lake of coffee soaking into Otto's pant leg. Peter took three quick steps forward and knelt down next the blue over-alled hull of a man he barely knew.

"Otto! Otto! Are you still here?"

Otto lay on his side with his right arm pinned under his head sticking straight above him and his left hanging limply over his chest. He could not even turn his head and as he struggled to open his eyes Peter could see the left lid drooping down like a wet leaf. He imagined the fall, slow almost comical. He could see the cup sliding off the saucer, bounding over the lake of the spill and into the other room. He could see the two trunks of Otto's legs waiver in the wind, the agonizing descent of the twisting torso, and the whipped slap of his hands on the floor in front of the stove like the final elastic bounce of tree limbs crashing in the forest.

He saw it all in his mind, but he could not hear it. His thoughts did not register a sound. It made him wonder if any clatter or a thud reverberated from the fall of a man. *Did it happen quickly or come too slowly?* So slow that the syllables of death spoke only in the decibels of a wilting flower that shrinks quietly from the sun.

"Pay-ter," bubbled weakly from Otto's mouth like heat from the core of the earth escaping through a pot of mud. Peter leaned in to understand these final words of such an intense man.

"I'm here Otto. What can I do?"

"Burn," Otto forced out.

Peter's first thought jumped to Holocaust. He remembered the tales of this hideous man and began to feel that Otto's last call rang through to the only Jew he knew. Peter suspected that he would absorb the final rays of one man's hate who would lay cursing 'til the end, but Otto's eyes did not leak. They barely opened and Peter saw none of yesterday's fire in those cataract orbs. The guileless intensity of those black pupils rested behind the approaching cloud of death.

Otto's chest expanded shakily. He focused his last strength on gathering air. "Hlet no ᵥun find me," he whispered. Peter knew these words no longer lashed out in violence toward him or the enemies of the past. These words spoke only surrender. "Burn," Otto swallowed, "Me." His eyes gave one last flicker of heat as he forced out his final word and then like his fall he puffed out, not a sound.

Peter straightened, put his hands on his knees and stared blankly straight ahead. He contemplated his work. When his eyes snapped back with resolution he set himself to the struggle of lifting. The unruly body weighed like an overfilled arm load of small logs that Peter had once carried into the kitchen. The seasoned logs carried less weight than they appeared, but they rolled and tumbled off the top. Peter continually stacked the limp limbs back across the load and carried the body out of the kitchen. He chose a wooden bench to set Otto down and Peter went back to the kitchen. He wiped up the lake of the spill and all the small ponds that tracked away from it. He righted the cup on the dining table.

He searched quickly around the stove before grabbing a small red tin resting next to the salt. He set off past the bathroom into a small room that was the brightest in the house. The windows opened up to the overrun garden and let in enough light to read the stacks of newspapers lining the baseboards around the empty room. He climbed up the narrow stairs and ducked into the tiny bedroom. He shook the blankets off the small twin bed and pulled the mattress out of the frame.

It took several trips and Peter's muscles felt unusually tired. The bundles of newspapers wore him down the most. Their brittle yellow pages and grainy black photos crumpled easily in his hands. He crushed them into loose balls that he tucked in and around the corners of his pile. Each clipping felt like Peter's story that he did not have the power to tell. He could not remember them, amnesia, and here he knelt pulling pages as if from his own journal to crush into the pile, but he continued.

When the pyre rose complete like a pyramid to a great leader in the middle of the room Peter picked up the red tin from a nearby table. He popped open its hinged lid and dumped out half a dozen matches. He pinned two together and tapped them lightly on the wall to equal out their lengths. He dragged them along the floor until friction brought them to flame. He lit them for his fathers and touched them to the papers until they began to burn his own fingers. He took two more and lit them for Otto's unborn children. Finally, Peter moved to the cool side of the heating stack of fire. He grasped the last two matches one in each hand. He took one for Otto and one for himself and slowly scratched their red self-loathing heads to life. He brought them together before he held them to the edge of a black ink picture of someone screaming hate in the face of another.

As the heat grew, Peter stepped away. In a minute the room flamed too hot to bare and he retreated, walking backwards outside into the woods. He stood watching the small building while the red-devils danced themselves out inside, but first they clung to the walls. Soon they jumped to the ceiling. In time that Peter could not measure the black tar shingles of the roof began to melt and drip away like shedding rain.

The pressurized silence of the moment ended with a frantic scratching near the peak of the roof. A stained pane of glass shattered in the heat and flame began to curl around the eaves. At the point of the roof the scratching turned to panicked chatter that ended in the whomp of two black faced raccoons jumping to the forest floor. They glanced dazed with fear at

Come Not To Us

Peter before they scampered off in the opposite direction, but not before Peter turned away.

He walked quietly to his car and rolled slowly around the two-tracked drive under the crab apple trees. He stopped next to the sign. He lowered his window to read once again without the glare of the glass.

!! PILGRIM !!
WHOEVER YOU ARE
FROM WHERE YOU COME
WHAT EVER YOU WANT
COME NOT TO US
GO HOME AND MAKE
SOMEONE ELSE HAPPY
OTTO AND ANNA

Peter looked back over his shoulder and could see the white smoke of the burning house curling up through the dense envelope of green. He did not second guess the building he decided to burn. It made sense for now. He removed his foot from the brake and the car rolled forward picking up speed on the road. He brought his attention to what lay ahead through his windshield and smiled as he spoke.

"Shtraight zu Hell."